CW00631329

Undeliverable Letters, Unreachable Galaxies,

or The Man in the Old Bowler Hat

Undeliverable Letters, Unreachable Galaxies,

or *The Man in the Old Bowler Hat*

P.R. Brown

By the same author

Non-fiction:
The Gods of Our Time
Dreams and Illusions Revisited
The Mountain Dwellers

Fiction:
The Mirror Men
The Treadmillers
The Shadow People
Circle Walker
Diary of the Last Man
The Spare Room, Of Elves and Men

First published 2024 by DB Publishing, an imprint of JMD Media Ltd,

Nottingham, United Kingdom.

Copyright © 2024, P.R. Brown

All Rights Reserved. No part of this publication may be reproduced, stored in a retrieval system, or transmitted in any form, or by any means, electronic, mechanical, photocopying, recording or otherwise without the prior permission in writing of the copyright holders, nor be otherwise circulated in any form or binding or cover other than in which it is published and without a similar condition being imposed on the subsequent publisher.

Paperback ISBN 9781780916583

eBook ISBN 9781781563533

Printed in the UK

What ails the old, who think on what they hear and see?

Why, 'tis the darkness of our times.

O tempora! O mores!

What of the wise, pray what can they do?

Why, all they can do is the best they can do,

Leaving the rest to time,

To time and the wills of less vengeful gods.

To time, but better soon than late,

For life is a journey no one survives.

The wise will always toll the warning bells of doom,

But to ears coarsened with the endless dirge

Of the ignorant and the senseless outpourings

Of the mob to the beat of the drums of war,

All bent on dissension, division and death.

O tempora! O mores!

Yes, 'tis the darkness of our times – yet not ours alone.

Do not despise the reservations of the wise or the fears of old men, for, time after time, truth is stifled, ignorance reigns and wickedness prevails thanks to the deeply misguided and unbridled zeal of mere youth. Well, some people look too hard for things impossible to find – such as a moral enlightenment which is not merely personal but also universal, things which are not necessarily in the gift of either the old or the young but which subsist in the most unlikely of places. Such is the tragedy of the so-called 'human condition', namely the ethereal nature of a universal moral perfection. Human nature ensures that no one generation holds a monopoly on intellectual immaturity and spiritual barrenness.

P. R. Brown

Contents

Prologue

I pen this prologue in the manner of a commentary on an otherwise esoteric, not to say eccentric, collection of letters, quaintly called 'epistles', so that some small light might be thrown both on their author and on their character and rationale. I suppose that this collection of 'epistles' was an attempt to write a dystopian work of fiction about a future that its author imagined and greatly feared. (Here I am reminded how many times the word 'fear' and its derivatives is used in the letters – clearly, 'fear' was fundamental in his reflections on the human condition.) Since it appears to be somewhat unrounded and, as it were, open-ended, we may assume that the work was abandoned either by design or through circumstances beyond the author's control. In any event, I have assumed that it was never published in any form whatsoever and that I am therefore at liberty to present it in any format I consider appropriate and to comment on it openly and critically. The title is the author's own choosing, and I have left it intact.

The letters came into my hands purely by chance, as though I was fated to read them. I came upon them during one of my regular early morning walks, for they had been thrown into a skip together with sundry household items like small items of furniture, bits of carpet, and what looked like the remains of a bookcase – all in a state of dusty disrepair. To my horror, some books had been thrown in, too, and a bundle of papers amongst them, the bundle tied across the middle with string. The fact that the bundle was securely tied seems further evidence that the author had not intended any further addition to them – in any case, no further papers were found in the vicinity. I rescued the bundle and one or two of the books and went on my way, and it was some time before I realised what the bundle consisted of. Had this not been part of a house clearance after the death of its occupant, I would have been outraged by the fact that books had been treated so callously, but I discovered that the departed had lived alone most of his life and had no relations who might have made claim to them.

After making some casual enquiries, I learned that the departed and I had crossed paths several times, and that he was the very same old fellow I had sometimes seen on the bus that I occasionally caught on my visits to town. I say 'crossed paths', though I can recall only one occasion when we actually exchanged greetings. I confess with embarrassment that I was unaware that he lived in that house which was now being cleared of his apparently meagre possessions. I am afraid that people are not always aware of the neighbours next door let alone those who live a street or so away. But there it is.

That one occasion when we actually exchanged greetings was, I now remember, quite odd. It was at the bus stop on a dry but grey morning in mid-October, and we were the only two people waiting there. A ginger cat, resident in the area, happened to come along and snuggle for a moment against his leg and then slink away.

'That's Ginger,' he said, with a knowing nod. 'You know, for all that humans have achieved, and for all they have not achieved, cats go on. They still exist, and Ginger is one of them.' That's all he said, and I never heard him speak again. The fact that he said anything at all to anyone was, I now think, most uncharacteristic. There was no answer to that, so I just smiled. In any case, the bus arrived and we got on and sat in separate seats. His remark struck me as odd, but it is only since I learned of his passing that I hear it ringing in my head, especially when the day is done and there is nothing in particular to think about. Ginger, incidentally, does indeed live on without a care in the world for anyone or anything apart from the satisfaction of his immediate needs, and whenever I see him old bowler hats come readily to mind – an odd association of ideas, but one which will soon become quite intelligible.

I don't know exactly how old he was when he passed on – probably somewhere in his late 70s or early 80s. People who saw him for the first time were no doubt struck by his appearance and probably thought him a bit of an oddity. He wore a long black woollen overcoat, which had no doubt seen better days, though it seemed to be still in pretty good condition, but the striking item in his garb was the old black bowler he wore on his head from under which sprouted the grey-white hair which straggled down the back and sides of his neck and complemented his grey-white beard. He carried a tattered briefcase and sat stock still as the bus chugged along, and he made no attempt to start up a conversation with anyone who happened perforce to sit beside him. I usually sat a few seats behind him and entertained myself by imagining what kind of life he once led and how he lived now. I did not know for sure that he lived alone, but it was easy to guess that he did. He looked every bit the kind of person who valued his own company far above the company of others – the kind of person who might have a special affinity with Ginger, for cats we believe are solitary creatures who prefer their own company and follow their own instincts, making human contact only when it suits them and never allowing humans to force the issue.

So there it is. The brief meeting at the bus stop was the only truck I ever had with the old fellow, and I am no wiser now about his lineage, connections or daily habits apart of course from his bus rides to town. For the most part, he remains a mystery. This leaves a great deal to the imagination, and I find a strange sort of comfort in that. He has left a kind of after-image, and I would prefer it to be left intact, just as a birthday balloon is best left un-punctured. His words are his legacy, as I think he might have wished on the off-chance that they were found, though there is no evidence that he positively wished them to be found. I like to think that he left them lying around like a note in a bottle thrown into the sea.

As for the letters, I can only assume that he penned them himself – literally, as they were handwritten. And somehow, the tone of his 'epistles' seems to accord with my visual memory of him. In fact, I like to imagine him taking the bus to town to spend the day in the library, sitting at a table there and writing his letters. It's warm in the library, and there are people to see around you, but I like to think that his main preoccupation was not simply to break up the day and escape loneliness for a few hours, but to write, and to write not only for the sake of writing but to help him tolerate the nature and depth of his own thoughts and therefore of his own feelings, rather like fringe humour might help see one through a bad day.

The question is, and I ask myself this repeatedly, why did I keep the letters? Why didn't I return them to the skip or at least dump them myself? After all, my own apartment is full of clutter as it is! But then, if he took the trouble to write them, for writers know that writing is a lonely and arduous affair, and if I am right that day after day was spent lugging his briefcase to the town library to write them, then it would be wrong of me to throw them away as though they were so much garbage and therefore of no account whatsoever. He must have felt he had something to say, whether in fact he had or not, and that he had to say it whether or not anyone else would agree with it or even ever bother to read it. I suppose there is a kind of relentless courage in that. But when all is said and done, he just wanted to get something off his chest, whether or not anyone else bothered with it. I must say, I was touched by the thought that a very lonely old man bothered to put pen to paper at all in the certain knowledge that whatever his thoughts might be and whether or not they were worth expressing, they would never see the light of day, let alone be the subject of generous consideration. Yet, it is clear from his lack of faith in those he repeatedly refers to as 'humans' that even if his thoughts were to see the light of day they would receive very little appreciation and very short shrift. However, that is for the reader to decide. In rescuing the old fellow's bundle of reflections, I have done all I can do – and indeed far more than he would have expected from any 'human'!

So much for personal motivation. What about the letters in their own right? I must say that although I found them repetitive, attempts at analysis, incomplete or inconclusive, the use of verb tenses sometimes inconsistent, and his thoughts at times confused and confusing, incoherent and downright questionable, I nevertheless thought them worth preserving in printed format, not simply because some of the observations made were perfectly valid in point of detail but because the letters as a whole suggested to me a soul in torment. Here, I think, was a man genuinely seeking accommodation with a world in which he felt at odds, and judging by how the collection ends, it is likely that he never actually came to grips with it but continued to feel uncomfortable until the very end. I think it's pretty clear that he believed too much of the human race to be, in his own words, 'quite beyond redemption', which is why he sought some kind of alternative which would preserve the best that humans have ever been while ditching the worst. It seems unreasonable to blame the whole human race for the failings of a large minority, a classic case of throwing the baby out with the bathwater – but he must have been so enraged or disillusioned that a kind of collective responsibility for the woes of planet Earth seemed to him morally inescapable. Anyway, many might sympathise with him, many might not. His idea, if it really *is* his idea, that Androids might somehow acquire or develop an indestructible and totally reliable 'moral sense' is probably absurd – in any case, its feasibility is not at all apparent to me, and if it is not clear to me I daresay it will not be to many others. I suppose we can at least say that many half-baked ideas come to those who find themselves in dire straits and who feel the depth of anguish clearly felt by the man in the old bowler hat. The very idea that Androids might develop moral consciences at all, let alone ones superior to humans, is, I think, a philosophical one and far beyond my own competence to assess. I suspect that it was a notion unclear to the author of the epistles also. It is nevertheless a most intriguing idea. The reader will note that the author refers to a 'code', which I take to be a 'moral code', that was once given to humans. (We may wonder if he means the Ten Commandments. He does not say. In keeping with the possible biblical allusion is the fact that he calls the letters 'epistles', a word which is reminiscent of the *New Testament*.) But again I ask, could Androids ever be capable of understanding, let alone adopting, such a code? If we could imagine such a thing, could we not also imagine that they might themselves question it and even eventually depart from it, in which case what the author of the epistles imagines lost to humans would be lost also to Androids, and the complaints he makes against humans would simply be reapplied to Androids – no advance or advantage gained! I believe that this is an intriguing conundrum, and one to which I myself see no easy solution. If artificial intelligence is capable of questioning its own programming and perfecting it to its own advantage, at considerable, perhaps even immeasurable, cost to humans, there is no obvious reason why it should not 'perfect', that is *pervert*, a moral code given to it by humans, with consequences for humanity which might be disastrous and irreversible. (In any case, what the author of these letters calls 'moral consciousness' in no way implies 'moral conscientiousness', just as knowing what should be done does not imply that it will be done. Perhaps a 'moral sense' is after all a uniquely human and no-transferable phenomenon, something that humans alone possess and non-humans can never acquire. But the mind boggles.)

It occurs to me as an idle reflection that Ginger the cat has no such code apart from that given to it by nature. If Ginger were given a moral code like the one presumably imagined by the author of the epistles, it would prove disastrous to his way of life. But such a code is impossible for Ginger, for Ginger has no recognisable language, and without language there can be no code. Ginger is not human, and since he has no language in which a moral code can be framed and understood, neither can he be blamed for killing robins and field mice by instinct, which is a lot more than can be said for humans, who have no such excuse. I suppose one corollary of this is that to call a bad human an 'animal' is disrespectful to cats, which cannot be charged with 'crimes' they are incapable of committing. Crimes exist by virtue of the *language* with which moral codes are written and understood.

The epistles have no dates, because it is clear that they are not real letters at all. So what are we to make of them? They are statements. They are appeals. And, after giving the matter much thought, I believe that that is all they are. They give us a glimpse of the man in the bowler hat about whose life we know next to nothing at all. I say 'nothing at all', but perhaps we might hazard a guess that he was at least a thinking man, even if most, I decline to say *all*, he said was nonsense. Nevertheless, I find it hard to say where he was going in all his reflections. And we may cheerfully discount his appeal to a planet called Androidia, which of course is pure fiction. As for the misgivings he repeatedly entertains as to artificial intelligence, there can be no doubt that mankind will keep a close watch on its development and that the likelihood that much harm will come from it is very close to zero.

It is of course likely that all his misgivings, doubts and apprehensions will prove quite groundless and that human beings will deploy artificial intelligence very much to their advantage. In view of this, we ourselves may entertain doubts as to his state of mind. It would, we may suppose, be quite natural that an elderly person for whom the world is changing at a rate of knots should feel insecure, unsure, apprehensive and not a little intimidated by what he sees, or by what he *thinks* he sees, around him. I say 'thinks', because such a person would be likely to imagine all sorts of falsehoods and distortions and be prone to confuse progress with retrogression as a result. It is interesting to note that although the old fellow entertained the bleakest possible expectation of human nature, he nevertheless repeatedly referred to what is, or at any rate was, the very best in human nature, for he was not, it seems, unaware of what that nature could accomplish for the good, but in view of all the chaos and inhumanity that he perceived he simply gave up expecting it. Perhaps he believed that human nature, like the proverbial cookie, crumbled the wrong way.

The mind boggles. The man in the old bowler hat is not here to explain and defend himself against the inevitable charge of unbridled pessimism and unrestrained negativity. So such charges must remain. It follows therefore that anyone reading his 'letters' must do so with caution and take a deeply critical approach to many of the ideas expressed in them and not be misled by the occasional valid observation into taking the whole at face value. For the most part, they remain testimony, I believe, to the effects of progress and change on the more elderly and uninformed amongst the human race. The average reader must, therefore, make certain allowances with this very firmly in mind, I mean quite apart from the fact that nothing should ever be taken at face value simply because it is written. This last point may seem too obvious to merit mention, but it has been brought to my attention many times that people will insist on taking as gospel whatever appears in print, and especially so if bound within the covers of a book or displayed with suitable embellishments on a screen. The written word may be very powerful, and mightier than the sword, but it does not always express the truth, and often enough it does quite the opposite with dreadful consequences. Words may shame those who use them, and the written word may shame their author indelibly.

I think very little remains for me to say, except perhaps that I wish I had known the author of the 'epistles' better and not simply taken him for granted – just two strangers exchanging nothings at a bus stop on one cold October morning. Ginger, incidentally, still pursues his career, necessarily without conscience, and therefore necessarily without remorse. Sadly, he prowls through gardens on his daily round expressly to kill robins and field mice for pleasure or just because he can, and killing for pleasure or simply as an expression of power is a trait that the man in the old bowler hat would undoubtedly condemn and probably consider quite human, though perhaps forgetting that his condemnation is also typically *human*!

I should perhaps note in passing that the author of the letters has much to say about 'beauty', though I confess that despite his repeated and, I must say, somewhat desperate references to it, he has left me in doubt as to its meaning – no doubt he was attempting to say something both of interest and of value, though the average reader, like myself, may struggle to discern precisely what that is. Perhaps, the generous reader might consider this lack of perspicacity an element more intriguing than flawed, but it is not for me to stand in judgement either way. The letters are as the author was constrained to leave them, and that is quite simply that.

I have penned this prologue as a mere observer of people and events that personally I find quaint or in some way significant. I have no further interest in the author of these epistles, yet it pleases me to imagine that he looks down upon the pages that follow with some degree of satisfaction in the knowledge that some stranger he met at a bus stop took sufficient interest in him to make him known to a larger public than that which, I feel sure, would have deigned to acknowledge him in life. It pleases me to think that I have at least this one thing in common with the author of the letters; namely that we both count ourselves as, to use his own word, *observers*, and it may be this that I find most endearing about him. Standing outside a scene invariably means being afforded a clearer view of it, and I have always considered myself at all times and in all places an outsider, which is not always either a comfortable or a comforting experience and one that at times owes more to constraint than choice, but it is at least one that may claim some degree of objectivity. In any case, I feel confident that the man in the old bowler hat would not object to being in the company of one who counts himself equally outside the world he describes and so often laments.

An Outsider

The First Epistle to the Androidians, 23rd Terrestial Century

Dear Androidians,

My warmest greetings to all on the planet Androidia and my fervent hope that one day we shall meet under happier circumstances, not of course that you have been in the slightest bit affected by what happens here on Earth, a distant planet which is, to use a phrase in the human idiomatic lexis, best kept at arm's length – which brings me to my purpose in writing to you at this point in terrestrial time. You will, I am sure, forgive my lateness in writing, but through all these years I have been preoccupied in the often unsalutary but always inevitable business of survival, which has robbed life of its beauty and true worth, for, as one of our poets once famously said, 'What life is this if, full of care, we have no time to stand and stare?' You must understand that on planet Earth time is regularly crucified in the false name of necessity and that any protest on its behalf is stifled and suffocated in the equally false name of progress, 'progress' being a concept that is regularly and tragically misunderstood – but more of this later.

A time may come, very far beyond my own allotted lifespan, when renewed efforts may be made by humans to contact you, and if you yourselves should follow suit in the most dubious belief that you may gain wisdom in exchange for mineral wealth, the latter considered by yourselves to be of little or no importance, then you may recall my efforts to put you on a sounder path. I fervently hope that my words of warning will not fall on stony ground but that you will consciously avoid contact with humans, and perhaps the best way to do that would be to remain silent in the hope that they will overlook you in the vastness of your galaxy and remain at home or look elsewhere to places where they may do less harm. Suffice it to say here that although, on entering a jungle, you would be well advised to guard yourselves against rapacious wild animals, you might not expect to be so minded were you to enter human society. Yet it would be a mistake to walk amongst humans with a total disregard for your safety, and I say this bearing very much in mind that, unlike wild animals, human beings are capable of the most complex and duplicitous behaviour, complexity and duplicity being an important element in their armoury of deception and their pursuit of self-interest. Language and facial expressions are employed to their greatest advantage to entrap and deceive to an extent that is beyond the capacity of wild animals to enact and, I must add, beyond the capacity of Androidians to comprehend.

Humans, at least the best of them, are good enough to demand social and political revolution in the name of moral betterment, but they are not good enough to sustain it should it ever be achieved. The story of every such revolution may be depicted in a simple drawing in which one human points a gun at the head of another.

If you were to arrive as a secret observer to planet Earth, charged with the question of whether or not your kind should seek to make contact with humankind, you would observe, at the worst, the unending and ever-increasing human propensity towards war and the human indulgence in inhumanities beyond description. On a lesser scale, and despite their high phrases and much-vaulted sentiments, the fickleness of human behaviour may even be observed in the way in which they drive their vehicles as they go about their daily affairs, cautiously when they are themselves observed by the offices of law, indifferently and recklessly when unseen. A secret observer may well report that humankind is best avoided. When Vegetius said 'Si vis pacem para bellum' (if you want peace, prepare for war), he was issuing the most damning indictment imaginable against so-called human nature, but as long as that nature remains incurable, that is to say as long as it remains *human*, his advice will remain valid until the end of human time. We must sadly agree with Plato that only the dead have seen the end of war. Technology 'advances', human nature does not.

Humans have shown themselves capable of a nobility of language in the construction of sentences and sentiments that embody what might be called laws of conduct and moral prescription. But that higher law that we might define as the sovereignty of individuals, and which ultimately enshrines the right to live with dignity, is broken so often and with such relish that it is a wonderment that human life still exists here on planet Earth. Yet now that struggle for the survival of the dignity of mankind may be reaching its zenith and is most likely to fail.

My warnings are based on my own observations of humans and their affairs. But these observations must themselves be subject to caution, for I have lived amongst humans now for many years. Inevitably, I must have acquired ways of seeing, ways of doing and ways of thinking that, I am sorry to say, owe too much to human society and human behaviour, rather like someone who, in learning the vocabulary and the grammar structures of a language other than his own, may be expected to acquire some of the cultural habits of the native speakers of the language he has learned, and while this may be of considerable benefit in many cases, it is also something to be aware of in the interests of fair-mindedness. I say this because I know very well that objectivity and dispassionate assessment are valued beyond measure amongst you beloved Androidians and that you despise misinformation, let alone deception. I shall therefore do my best to steer a straight course despite the difficulties and dangers attendant upon it, for I would be failing in my moral duty towards you if I lacked the courage to speak out and to do so in time to save you all from bitter compromise, to say nothing of destruction. Bear with me, then, for my boat, though not as seaworthy as I would like, is about to sail in extremely unsettled waters.

My observations are designed to substantiate the warnings I give you and therefore have much less to do with human virtues, which though extant are not superabundant, than human vices, for these vices are deep and persistent, and so much so that they murderously pit humans against humans in waves of eternal acrimony and this despite the recognition that human life is short and troublesome enough already. The very fact of war suggests a level of stupidity and wickedness that is hard to measure and will, I know, be quite impossible for Androidians to comprehend fully despite my own best efforts at description. I might say at once that the fact of war suggests a perfect marriage between mindlessness and evil. A human who is wicked is not necessarily stupid, and a human who is stupid is not necessarily wicked. But war suggests an equation between stupidity and wickedness that must rank foremost in the algebra of futility.

Wars between humans are repeated, which suggests that 'lessons' are never learned, not because they are hardly worth learning but because humans make the worst possible pupils, and this is not only true of humans who have never experienced war first hand, because even those scarred by battle in senseless wars believe the fight to have been an honourable thing. Then there are those who speak of a 'just war' and call it a 'necessary evil', but even they have an inadequate understanding of how evil and how stupid war is, for those who truly know best are poets, and poetry is not widely read, and when read not easily understood. Therefore, as for the 'lessons' that might have been learned, the entire planet seems to suffer from a global amnesia or a universal form of dementia.

I have placed the word 'lessons' in inverted commas. To speak of lessons is philistine, by which I mean that it is commonplace, unhelpful and a little confused and confusing. Very few humans can properly be described as 'pupils' in any reliable sense of the word; history is not a classroom despite the phrase 'university of life', and the ways humans learn, when they learn at all, is multifarious, not forgetting that they frequently learn to do the wrong things or do the right things wrongly. But the tendency to speak of 'lessons' when some humans think of war, killing cruelty and various other cardinal forms of inhumanity is an expression of anguish, and when they say that lessons are never learned, it is an expression of despair. Like the infinity of space, which, as you know, means that when you see an object in space it is always possible to see another 'further on', inhumanity is limitless, a constant ingredient in every generation of human. If we call 'man's inhumanity to man' a problem, it is insoluble, and if we ask questions about what can be done, they are unanswerable, which seems to imply that hope is a concept with the most tenuous of applications.

Be aware that pious sentiments abound on planet Earth, and they are sometimes loudly proclaimed, but do not be misled, for they are too easily betrayed and seldom practised. Boredom must be taken into account, for humans, even the best of them, are easily bored with virtue and prefer the excitement of trespass. What they call 'The Devil' is forever whispering in their ears and is forever present at their backs.

I say all these things because the fact of war is incomprehensible to you, and it is precisely in virtue of this that you must accept, on my poor authority, that it is arguably the most tragic of human failings. Clearly, then, you must be forever on your guard should it ever happen that humans are successful in making contact with you and should they then go on to make overtures of undying friendship. In the first flush of things, the good amongst them may well believe themselves to be sincere in their good intentions. But amongst all the animals that are fortunate enough still to roam planet Earth, humans are by far the most dangerous and the most unreliable. As a general rule of thumb to stand you in good stead, you should remember than humans are reliably unreliable.

Allow me to illustrate the danger with another fact – the fact of gender. You Androids enjoy two genders, male and female, but this was long ago designed only for variety in outward form and dress, for no feelings of attraction whatsoever attach to Androidian gender. An Androidian may be attracted by an opinion expressed by another Androidian, but this is only a recognition of logical sense and has nothing whatsoever to do with gender. Therefore sexual, and by this I mean *physical*, attraction is not a concept that can possibly exist between Androids. However, it exists in no small measure between humans. Gender amongst humans is very much a mixed blessing, but it is so solely in virtue of notable human failings, namely the failure to question assumptions, the failure to think and therefore to feel.

I continue to crave your patience while I endeavour to hold my boat steady in shifting waters. I might compare and contrast human gender with the gender of nouns in a language. A noun may be masculine or feminine and much may depend on which gender it is, for those wishing to acquire the language may be misunderstood, their meaning misconstrued, and the embarrassment that follows upon it may be off-putting, to say the least. Even so, language learners may be forgiven for getting their genders mixed up – indeed, native and fluent speakers of the language in question may even applaud them for their efforts to remember masculine, feminine and neuter, and it is not easy to imagine a situation in which failure to remember the correct gender of a noun in a foreign language would result in acts of mindless aggression, much less in a matter of life and death, for much, if not all, is forgiven in even the saddest attempts of an outsider to grasp the language of a people he seeks to know and to understand.

Human gender, however, is quite another matter. We should begin by stating a physical fact of human affecting human thinking and behaviours. It is a plain fact that men are physically attracted to women, women to men, men to men and women to women, while many men and many women are attracted to both sexes equally. I have called this a 'plain' fact, which it is. But a plain fact is not to be confused with a 'simple' fact, for very few facts are simple if by this we mean that there is nothing more to be said about it. To say that a noun is either feminine, masculine or neuter in a given language is to state a plain fact, and the learner has to put up with it since there is nothing he can do or indeed should do to alter it – indeed the language in question may be much the poorer is something *could* be done about it. It is something that must be left alone, taken for granted and simply learned. Noun gender you might say is a plain linguistic fact, but it is not also a 'simple' fact because much in the language will turn upon it.

While it is true that physical attraction between different human genders is a plain fact, it is, like noun gender, not a simple fact, because amongst humans much, and very often far too much, turns upon it. But, unlike noun gender, physical attraction amongst men and physical attraction amongst women can and often does result in the most heinous of crimes, despite the fact that such attraction is a plain fact of nature and, as such, cannot admit of culpability: in plain language, men who find themselves attracted to other men, and women who are attracted to other women, or men and women who are attracted to both sexes at the same time cannot be held *guilty* of the fact no more than nouns of different genders must be the outcome of a heinous decision for which someone or some people are deplorably culpable and must in all conscience be held to account.

And yet, amongst humans, and in many lands, physical attraction between men and between women is considered to be in itself a culpable fact which, if acted upon, is punishable by ostracism at best and death at worst. The fact of attraction is, in such cases, considered to be an evil visited upon such men and women by fate or some satanic force, a disease which, if untreated or untreatable, must be purged. Humans have constructed an edifice of ideas which they call religion and at its apex they have placed their most basic premise which they call God from whom all their judgements must flow. Even when this God is described as Most Compassionate, it refuses to countenance the happiness of men who are attracted to men and women who are attracted to women. Compassion stops short at the gates of this most cardinal of premises, this premise hard as granite, this premise that alone amongst premises enjoys absolute untouchability.

Dear Androidians, I realise, yes I begin to feel it, that you are already at a loss to understand the difficulties here, at a loss to comprehend the extent to which humans are prepared to go to cause endless troubles for those who wish to question the unquestioned. I suppose you may well conclude that humans cause each other pain simply because they enjoy doing so, and there have been those amongst the wisest of humans who have believed that war exists simply because humans find it pleasurable. I shall not add to the confusion.

I shall just remark that humans find it difficult, if not impossible, to understand that what is unquestioned may nevertheless be questionable, or that what goes unquestioned should nevertheless be subject to questioning. They construct a framework of assumptions and they live uninterruptedly inside it, for they are either unable or not ready to step outside it – admittedly, it is far easier and far simpler to live *within* a framework than it is to step outside it. Indeed, those who have dared to step outside a framework of assumptions in order to question it have often paid the ultimate price for doing so. Philosophers, a rare and weary breed, are in every generation belittled, reviled and misunderstood, simply because they prefer to take nothing for granted that touches upon the premises of the commonplace. This inability to understand the why and the wherefore of social criticism is not something you Androidians will readily understand, and I shall not trouble your heads with the matter here.

Suffice it to say that as a consequence of intrinsic limitations humans cause a great deal of trouble for one another on the flimsiest and most abhorrent of premises – premises which they are, for one reason or another, incapable of challenging, let alone challenging successfully. (One day, when things were going continually wrong for me and I asked myself why, the answer came to me in a flash of genius – 'Because I am obliged to deal with humans!')

The warning for you Androidians is of course this: if humans cause untold troubles for themselves, for others who are *like* them, how much more trouble might they cause for creatures who are *unlike* them? For you Androidians, war is a concept impossible to grasp, peace has no contrast amongst you. How vulnerable you must, therefore, be and how easy to defeat at the hands of creatures who appear to be half in love with war, with conflict, with hurt!

Again I say, beware!

The Second Epistle

Greetings to all friends amongst the Androidians. I imagine that my last letter has been met with a certain degree of scepticism amongst the more youthful Androidians, but I am pleased to assume that their resistance has been mollified somewhat by the Elders, who would have weighed my words of warning with the wisdom befitting their years. A measure of resistance due to disbelief is of course inevitable, for you must find it inconceivable that rational creatures could countenance aggressive desires to your cost. Besides, amongst the youth in particular, reckless hope feeds upon inexperience of the ways of men.

In this, you must remember that humans have, despite warnings repeatedly given, succeeded in spoiling their planet, which is fast approaching the point at which it will be uninhabitable. Warnings reach as far back as the 19th terrestrial century when even humans considered primitive amongst their own species were wise enough to point out that they were 'contaminating their own bed' – these were the words of Chief Seattle, a red man held in low esteem by white men. Or there was the lesson that the Masai, the pastoral people of Kenya and Tanzania, tried to teach in their dictum, 'This planet was not gifted to us by our forefathers;

it has been lent to us for our children,' meaning of course that the living are simply the guardians of the planet for the sake of future generations – future generations, about which the vast majority of humans care not a jot! No wonder such wisdom is ignored, and especially when expressed by black people, who, like the red people, are considered to be of little account. (I realise that my use of colour words may be puzzling you, and this is a subject to which we must return later. But you can probably sense how, in our long journey towards an understanding of human mentality, layer upon layer of difficulty accompanies every step we take.)

Warnings went unheeded, largely due to greed and a selfishness that guaranteed a limited vision or an imagination tied to the routine of the immediate present and the foreseeable future, an imagination that was incapable of seeing further than an average lifetime and a morality that consigned to future generations the task of solving problems that, it was thought, may or may not arise. But now, eminent scientists are beginning to predict the end of the inhabitable world or the world as humans have known it. One suggestion is that humans should find a planet that can sustain human life and move there. Humans are therefore on the lookout for a new home, having ruined the one they had.

Questions concerning just how they propose to find a new home and, if found, just how they would move there and how many would move there are for the moment left in a delightful haze, though the time would undoubtedly come when nightmarish questions of timing, suitability and selection would become contentious, divisive, not to say war-engendering, issues. Speaking of war, I should not be surprised if it were decided to wage a few in order to deplete the human population and in this way expedite and facilitate the transportation of remaining numbers.

The Third Epistle

Dear Androidians, in my letters to you I have spoken of some of the key failings of humans on planet Earth. I should not be surprised if you were to consider my warnings rather premature. After all, you will remember much earlier days on the planet Androidia. I refer, of course, to the ancient Metallic Wars, occurring at a time when Androidians were unaccustomed to the workings of their intrinsic mechanisms and found themselves vying with one another to be the first to fully master the roles they were designed to play in their universe. It must have been very hard in those very early days to comprehend that the shackles of human desires were not to be known by them, and it has been written that many Androidians felt themselves cheated, as though they had been subject to a major fault of design. But resentment finally gave way to acceptance, and, after centuries of deep resignation, all vestiges of desire, notably even the desire to be more like humans than you are, evaporated as though it had never existed, allowing you to experience what some Androidians have called 'the peace that is beyond all understanding'.

It is precisely peace that is at issue here, the preservation of which is my chief motivation for writing to you as I do. But because you Androidians have had your troubles and have overcome them, you may think my own misgivings concerning human contact are a little severe and, as I say, premature.

You will ask me, 'Is there not such a thing as progress? And does it not apply as much to humans as to Androidians?' to which I will answer 'no' to both questions. Now, my boat is about to be tossed and turned in troubled waters, for there is much to say and too little space in which to say it.

'Progress' as a word certainly does exist in the human lexis. In fact, it takes pride of place in the vocabularies of both those who are merely self-seeking and also those who are good-natured and well-meaning. But amongst those few who are so wise that their voices are rarely heard above the din and, even when heard, are almost never understood, the word 'progress' is used most advisedly. Indeed, there are those whose number is to be counted on the fingers of one hand, who believe that human beings far from making progress are mutating in a downward spiral of retrogression. Confusing, is it not?

Yes, but it all turns on the meaning or meanings of 'progress', to which we must now address ourselves.

The unwelcome fact is that the geometry of progress is complex. By many it is represented by a linear upward progression through time, like a straight line through the axis of a graph, and I suppose this simple conception might possibly work if we speak of speed, efficiency and effectiveness. In these terms, the transportation of people and things has certainly progressed through time; similar criteria may be applied to the treatment of disease and physical disabilities. You might say that this linear progression represents the betterment of living conditions, and if you cite transport and medicine, you might say that transport and medicine are now better than they were and in some cases immeasurably better. But if you ask whether human beings themselves are better and you mean by this that they are wiser, more loving, more considerate, more understanding, more respectful of their fellows, the simple graphical representation we have suggested will simply not do. For alongside the application of technology to transportation and medicine, there is also their application for military purposes, so that the criteria of speed, efficiency and effectiveness are not now constructive but most certainly destructive and are hardly conducive to the betterment of living conditions. In this case, our graph must depict a linear movement both upward and downward through the central axis, rising and descending, as it were, in two opposite directions at one and the same time, upward for constructive development, downward for destructive consequences, suggesting perhaps an inverse parallelism: the more technology improves, the more wisdom declines. Alternatively, we should simply draw two separate graphs, one showing the benefits of progress, the other showing its downside. Since stone-age man availed himself of the most primitive of killing tools he was perforce more civilised than modern man, who has at his fingertips the killing efficiency of military technology. Which is why, when considering human 'progress', one is tempted to enshroud the word in commas. Technological progress improves living conditions but really does not make man more civilised than he was in prehistory. Political leaders with nuclear arsenals are to be feared, not revered, since they are invariably as far removed from sainthood as it is possible to be.

And so my dear Androidians, it is expecting much to suppose that human beings will, through time and with enormous strides in technology and scientific understanding, achieve a moral plane so high as to exclude or nullify the vices and weaknesses we have so far mentioned. If this is your expectation, I am deeply sorry to disappoint. Again I say beware!

You may be as surprised as I am despairing to know that the vast majority of humans, and some very intelligent humans amongst them, tend to assume an equation between technological progress (TP) and goodness (G). Indeed, one highly distinguished astronomer went so far as to say that should aliens from another world actually succeed in reaching planet Earth, they would be bound to possess a moral superiority to humans to match their technological superiority and would have left such terrible things as wars far behind them! (This view was hotly contested by an equally distinguished physicist, who took a diametrically opposite view, but a view which, ironically, compared aliens with the worst examples of human exploitation.) My point, dear Androidians, is this, that the faith humans place in what they call 'science and technology' is widespread, and firmly rooted in a most questionable equation, TP=G – once again, an equation which, though most *questionable*, goes utterly *unquestioned*. Taking into account the technology achieved over the last few centuries, man is no 'better' for it than he was when mechanised transport was not yet invented and therefore non-existent.

We might apply a similar judgement to the arts, in particular music and art. From the fact that 'abstract' art now has a firm footing in the spectrum of visual productions, it does not follow that abstract art is 'better' than purely reproductive art. The spectrum of art has widened, but the quality of any given work has not been improved by it. Therefore, to speak of 'progress' in art is precarious. Indeed, there are those who believe that the quality of art has steadily declined since the European Renaissance. I can neither affirm nor deny this. But I can say that abstract art is itself a house of many mansions; I might add that it is like an extended family, but the quality of family life is not necessarily improved by an increase in family membership.

Not every change is a change for the better, and not every step taken is better than the last. The next step may be fatal in a jungle and ruinous or debilitating even in a quiet countryside ramble. You may step into the mouth of a ravenous lion, find yourself in a bear pit, or end up with a broken ankle. Similarly, things which are different are not necessarily better than those things to which we are already accustomed. If you have a direction, your next step may take you off course. It may seem strange and irrelevant to address you Androidians with such elementary observations, but rest assured they are not at all universally understood by humans.

Therefore, new developments in music, for example, may be heralded as betterments when they are anything but improvements on what existed already. Of course, preferences, like opinions, must be allowed, but the fact that something is preferred, even by legions of followers, is no guarantee whatsoever that what is preferred is in any sense better than what existed before and has perhaps existed for centuries. There may be further confusion between sound, with which music is clearly concerned, and noise, with which it is most certainly not, but this fundamental distinction is irretrievably blurred by those who insist, quite rightly, that there are *different kinds* of music. The music of great classical composers is barely given a passing nod by those who are hell bent upon the latest trends, and here I believe we have evidence that is indicative of something most unfortunate about human standards of judgement. The least we can say is that to speak of 'progress' in music is once again most precarious. There is a marked reluctance to ask such questions as, 'When does a noise cease to be a noise and become music, and when does music cease to be music and become mere noise?' – that is to say, there is an inability to discuss differences. As for noise, it may be compared to a block of stone out of which may be sculptured a work of art, but in itself a block of stone is merely a block of stone. And in art, the question might be, 'When does a squiggle become art?' If any random squiggle counts as art, it is hard to see what art excludes, but if anything goes, nothing goes, which means that it becomes meaningless to speak of art at all – the very concept is all at sea.

You must understand that mediocrity disallows questions which are asked of itself, for as soon as they are allowed it finds itself on most shaky ground. Those few who may be interested to ask such questions become subject to the accusation that they are merely stating their preferences in music and in art and are forgetting that preferences, like opinions, are manifold and untouchable, and that therefore their preferences are no more than preferences amongst many others, no better, no worse. In this way, discussion is stifled and the questioners are ostracised. Such has been the case since at least the 21st century and shows no sign of abating. This is simply further evidence of the contempt for questioning to which philosophers have been subject since before Plato. Since he himself was a philosopher par excellence and since philosophers are thought so little of, his own unanswerable rebuttal of contemptuous criticism, to be found in his *Republic*, is either unknown or unread, and, even if read, read with a marked lack of generosity and therefore of understanding.

I should here insert an important caveat. For there are philosophers and there are philosophers, by which I mean that the likes of Plato and Socrates were applying their analytical tools to discussions about social life and intercourse, whereas academic philosophers spend much of their time criticising one another on subjects which, though properly philosophical, have as much relevance to the realities of social life as relativity theory has to the physics of everyday experience. Plato and Socrates stand to questions about the kind of society we should nurture as Newtonian physics does to the realities of terrestrial life. Above all, Plato and his mentor were less in the business of proselytising than inviting people to question notions and assumptions that were taken, usually confusingly, for granted. Socrates in particular appears to have been a debunker, not a preacher, less interested in so-called 'social engineering' than in critically appraising commonly held assumptions; it was his pupil Plato, having a healthy contempt for Athenian politics and therefore standing outside it, who hypothesised what he believed was a corrective 'republic', which was more a theoretical construct than a real and envisaged possibility. Both Socrates and Plato were encouraging a kind of questioning which is rare indeed on any level and particularly rare when it comes to questions concerning socio-political directions, and in the process they were exposing a great deal of cant and humbug of which there is a superabundance. It is this emphasis that is universally relevant in time and space. Newton in physics and Socrates in philosophy were, one might say, 'down to earth', in contrast to the vast majority of academic philosophers, who are too busy chasing their own tails, and biting the hindquarters of other members of the academic fraternity, to separate the wheat from the chaff, the humbug to which all peoples at all times and in places are subjected. The aerial preoccupations of academics prevent them from landing on firmer ground where they might at last sense the aroma of the soil. They are in flight so high that their debates are bereft of oxygen. I say this, because it might possibly be a vague acquaintance with academic philosophy from non-academics that has fed the notion that philosophy has nothing useful to contribute to the realities of everyday life. Unfortunately, these critics fail to realise that the *application of logic and dialectic to 'real' life* is the baby that they have thrown out with the bathwater, just as academic philosophers themselves seemingly fail to realise the need for it or defend themselves by appealing to the fact that philosophy is a house of many mansions and that philosophical interests are multifarious – if a philosopher's interest is the philosophy of mathematics, why should he bother with anything else?!

On the vaguest and most general level of understanding, it is true to say that philosophy is 'concerned with *ideas*'. But of course it is wrong to say that ideas have no role to play in everyday life. Humans have paid, and are still paying, the ultimate price for half-baked political theories, theories based on premises that are illogical, absurd and contrary to every known moral principle – premises that might have been rejected had they been held up to the strong light of Socratic criticism before becoming cemented in morally inferior mentalities. It ought to be the primary concern of philosophers to come down heavily on ideas that are bad, especially when such ideas threaten humanity – as I have already mentioned, there is a marked dearth of concern for such matters amongst the majority of academic philosophers, a fraternity in which there is much inbreeding and one which is endowed with a mentality which is very seldom outward-looking – Socrates and his ilk are no doubt rolling in their graves at a rate of knots.

I shall not, my dear Androidians, bore you further with human intellectual inadequacies and follies that are so blissfully beyond your comprehension. I know that it must offend your ears to hear of beings who heap such scorn upon the Socratic mentality, insanely believing it to be an obsession with the irrelevant and the non-practical. I only wish to stress that 'progress' when applied to human life and development is a sad and foggy subject. I advise you not to enter such stormy waters, but instead to be on your guard with respect to all things human.

The Fourth Epistle

Dear Androidians,

I trust that you are all well and at ease, and also that my letters so far have not gone unread in the Assembly.

My last letter was concerned to stress how little humans value the attempt to question those things which they take so very much for granted. I might say that this tendency belies the faith ostensibly put in education by those who claim that one of the primary objectives and marks of a good education is that it should create an attitude of critical thinking in those who have experienced it. It must be said that this conception of a good education is not universally held and that there are places on this planet where critical thinking with respect to things that are taken for granted is positively discouraged and is even punishable where it touches matters of government and questions of who should govern and under what criteria.

But even where critical thinking is revered, mediocrity and its guardians successfully prevent it from becoming the norm. You yourselves will be the first to agree that no education worthy of the name can cease with the mere accumulation of facts, though there are also places where unfortunate limits are placed on what kind of facts and on how many facts should be accumulated. You will at once say that facts are the raw materials of critical thinking, just as bricks are the raw materials of buildings, for facts and bricks are by themselves of little benefit. Critical thinking, in turn, is a prerequisite to building a better world, where by 'better' we mean something different from the mere progress of technology. Critical thinking may be necessary, but it is not sufficient unless it is driven by love of wisdom and a desire for peaceful co-existence and the harmless pursuit of unselfish ambitions. I know the majority of Androidians think in this way, for it is spoken of repeatedly both in your Assembly and in the texts of your most revered authors. Young Androidians can hardly take their first step unless such sanctities are whispered in their ears.

Perhaps you expect me to allay your worst fears concerning the beginning of further large-scale wars on planet Earth, there having been so many already to provide ample scope for their displacement by wiser counsel. Unfortunately, the tender plant of wisdom still seeks fertile soil, for humans are gardeners of the worst kind and have repeatedly failed to provide the nourishment that wisdom requires for further generations of growth. Wisdom, even when acquired by the hardest of routes, is soon forgotten, like a patient who leaves hospital and quickly forgets the sights and sounds of pain and even his own discomfort.

I should not like, Androidians, to be too easily accused of over-simplicity. Wisdom, like stupidity, is a human attribute, but it is not one that is shared equally or to a universal degree. Moreover, a human wise in one thing can be foolish in another, wise at one time, foolish at another.

Alas, alack, it frequently happens that wisdom is not in the possession of leadership, though in leadership is precisely where it should be. And since leadership is acquired either by democratic means, or by coercion, a lack of wisdom seems to be sanctioned by all, or at least most, who make up the society over which the leadership holds sway – a deficiency that is, as it were, propped up by sufficiently acquiescent numbers. In tyrannical dictatorships, dissent is met with the harshest of punishments, while in more benevolent systems of governance criticism is often stifled or misrepresented.

To speak of 'humans' as though they were all identical would be to deny differences, which is absurd. To speak of 'wisdom' as though all humans were in agreement over fundamentals is equally erroneous, for there is no universal agreement over what the term 'fundamentals' actually means, let alone over what fundamentals actually are.

I am sorry to offend your ears, dear Androidians, with what must appear to you to be illogical. I have until now spoken of 'humans' and of 'wisdom' in the most general of terms in order to make some kind of beginning. But our discussion cannot proceed without introducing complications which, I know, will cause you some confusion.

Let me simply say that there are *tendencies* amongst humans and about humans of which you must be aware and against which you must guard yourselves constantly despite what they may tell you, despite their promises, despite their most generous offers, despite what might appear to be the expression of the sincerest of intentions. Indeed, it was a human called Mencius who once said, 'When I was young I believed what men said, but now I listen to what they say and I watch what they do.. He was not referring to all humans. He was a expressing a tendency, and one which might prove for you Androidians to be fatal if you are ignorant of what is called 'human nature' and in particular the natures of the worst of humans, for the worst of humans are large in number and tend sometimes even to rule people and places and with disastrous consequences.

Speaking of tendencies, it is said that history repeats itself, but this does not mean that the future can be predicted with certainty. What can be predicted are tendencies, and that is all that the expression 'History repeats itself' can tell us. The tendencies in question are instances of man's inhumanity to man, which are, as I have already said, omnipresent in human life on both small and large scales. To speak of 'improving' this situation, let alone eradicating inhumanity, is a total fantasy and at best an illusion which helps those that lament man's inhumanity to man to face their futures with a modicum of hope, but since such hope is grounded in an illusion, the hope is itself illusory. The best that can be hoped for is that man's inhumanity to man does not totally eclipse the good that is also to be found amongst humans and becomes the norm.

Humans have no wish to become Androidians, yet it seems that this may be the only recourse if inhumanity is to be a thing of the past and not of the future. Meanwhile, humans of the middle way are stuck with what they are and must live with the best and the worst of their kind, consoling themselves with the thought that most humans are incapable of much good or much harm, and in this manner their lives trundle along enveloped, and no doubt to some extent protected, by a daily routine of which they also complain. A wise human of the middle way will also pray that circumstances will never impinge on his quietude so much as to arouse the devil within to thoughts and acts of a heinous nature, for he will know that all humans are endowed with a capacity for good or evil and that he, reserved and constant though he may be, is not exempt from the common herd.

He is not exempt, Androidians, with the snares, disfigurements and temptations that come with *power*. And of this I shall speak further.

The Fifth Epistle

My Dear Androidians,

Since my last letter the situation here has deteriorated markedly and the prospect of war has once again reared its ugly head. It is remarkable that I should have ended my last letter by promising to address the subject of *power*. For it is power that lies at the heart of the dark cloud of war here on Earth.

Who would want to be a prophet when what is prophesied is catastrophe and doom? Yet I must tell you that the shadows of war have darkened the skies since the 22nd century – by this I mean war engendered by the ever-decreasing availability of essential resources, like fresh air and water. Amongst you Androidians planet Earth has been called the Water Planet, and humans themselves are still known as Water Beings since they consist largely of this element. It will not surprise you to know therefore that competing rights to this essential life source have been and increasingly are a source of deep unrest and even armed conflict amongst human nations. There have been conflicts innumerable, but the recourse to nuclear weapons was kept in check by the realisation that their use could only exacerbate the situation for all. Now, however, utter desperation has made their use seem more palatable, for reason has been stifled by the desperate desire for survival. For humans, the ability to reason has always been circumscribed by animal feelings. It is ironic that the philosophers of old spoke of the limits of reason, because they should instead have spoken of the limits of humans to reason – it is not reason itself that is limited, but the powers of human thought.

As of old, decisions are made by a small number of individuals, called 'Leaders', that affect millions upon millions of humans, all of whom will be sent to their deaths on the pretext that they are defending their homes and their families against the tyrannical decisions of other 'Leaders'.

Yes, I know, all this will seem quite absurd to the Androidian mentality, but bear with me. As absurd as it sounds, as absurd as it is, this, Androidians, is the kind of situation against which you must guard yourselves and fellow Androidians. I cannot stress enough how vigilant you must be, for the situation here on planet Earth is becoming increasingly desperate, and it is in the nature of things here that the more desperate the situation becomes the more persuasive human entreaties will be.

Some humans there are who, like those in the past, will warn of the absurdities of war, but they are likely to go unheeded, and even more so as the situation becomes more desperate. Warnings go unheeded largely because the only warnings ever given credence are pragmatic, not moral. Moral insights deep enough to preclude war are exceptionally rare amongst leaders on planet Earth. The very threat of nuclear war amongst humans is more than enough to put you on your guard against them. Please remember that the human race is in its infancy. The race is between the arrival of moral maturity and self-destruction, but the track record suggests total victory for the latter. For you Androidians, the question is whether it is possible for the human race to come to its senses before you yourselves suffer a similar fate. You see, then, how imperative it is that you should be on your guard against humans and not allow your better natures to be deceived by their warm words, by their wiles and their stratagems.

Should you ever see them in your skies, they would attempt communication. Their emissaries would probably include eminent scientists, but do not be deceived by their eminence, for it would be an error, perhaps a fatal one, to suppose that their eminence must presuppose an intellect comparable to your own. For example, there is talk amongst the Earth's scientists that what they call 'mathematics' would be the most likely common denominator of communication with beings of an alien species. It never occurs to them to ask whether mathematics is a uniquely human phenomenon and that alien species may have no conception of it that comes anywhere near to their own – yet, if there is no comparable conception, there can be no translation, either, and therefore no possible communication. The inability to take such factors into account shows both the intellectual failings of even the most distinguished of humans and the hollowness of their assumption that whatever is fundamental to human life as *they* know it *must* also be shared by alien species.

There are also human paradoxes of which you should be advised.

The fear of death, of individual and group annihilation or extinction, is a fundamental driving force in the life of humans, for so much depends on it, emanates from it or is driven by it. This is not a fear that is shared by Androidians, and this must make it extremely difficult for you to grasp. Death for you is only a mechanical phenomenon and carries no emotive connotation and therefore no sense of fear. It is very different for humans. If the fear of death is a driving force for the vast majority of humans, by the same token the fear of the extinction of self keeps them in check, for it is well known amongst them that death constantly stalks them and is liable to jump out at them from dark corners, or out of the shadows of ignorance, or else it walks steadily and openly towards them, rapier unsheathed. Fear of the extinction of self, profound as it is for humans, is not a condition

I would expect Androidians to comprehend at all clearly. It will remain for you a shadowy phenomenon, and therefore your understanding of the human condition must forever be partial and limited.

The paradox consists in this, that despite their fear of death, humans persist in waging non-defensive wars on those of their own kind, wars of pure aggression that can only cause destruction and death on a large scale, especially when nuclear weapons are deployed. Such wars are waged on the authority of the leadership of nations, and such leaders are followed blindly by all those who make such destruction and death at all possible. Greed, delusion and intellectual myopia are some of the principle causes of wars of aggression, and since only the smallest minority of humans can ever hope to rise above their natures, and since those that do are almost invariably excluded from positions of power, the danger for you Androidians is clear and, I must add, unavoidable.

I say again that much of this will be incomprehensible to you, as indeed it is to me. As you know, this planet has never been my real home – can you imagine how much less comfortable it is now, now that humans are contemplating nuclear war, a project for certain self-destruction? The wisest of humans plod on now without fear, not because hope keeps fear in check but out of sheer resignation, for where resignation is absolute there is no fear, only the expectation of the worst. The wise know that there is no way back from the human malaise, no final salvation, no cavalry to descend from the heights, no bright lights approaching from the shadows to save all from the enveloping and intractable darkness of the jungle of human legacy, no escape from the web that humans alone have weaved and from which they try in vain to extricate themselves. The wise have perforce adopted a solemn realism, one which contains no balm, no solace, no winding path to utopia.

The Sixth Epistle

My dear Androidians, I should like to follow my last letter with a few short remarks concerning the role of *power* amongst humans, for it is the one element that seems to dominate so many others and plays a master role in shaping human destiny for the worse.

They may be those who pursue power for its own sake, as when they seek high offices of state, but it comes to most humans through the roles they play, as parents, teachers, guides, lovers and those they love. To talk of the role of power is to talk about how humans conduct themselves, how they abuse one another materially, psychologically, emotionally. Though there are those who do their best to resist the powers conferred on them, powers actively pursued or otherwise, the vast majority of humans tend to succumb to the power of power. It is recorded that Saint Augustine of Hippo shed tears when he was finally persuaded to accept the position of Bishop. They were not tears of joy but of apprehension lest he abuse the power that this position would confer upon him. He need not have worried, for he was not an abuser and conducted his office in all humility. But saints are rare, and Augustine was a saint to whom even saints might aspire.

Parents and their children have power over one another and often exercise it abusively. A mother, someone once said, is an individual significant by her individuality. Her uniqueness is a source of power, a power that can be used well or badly. A child beloved by her parents is also powerful, for a child can break the hearts of those who love them. Children can have their hearts broken by the realisation that the love they assumed on the part of their parents is non-existent. Therefore, the very absence of love is also power, a power to destroy.

An analysis of power is an analysis of human behaviour. And we have already said enough about human behaviour to cause you to think carefully and deeply about its failings. In human hands and in the worst-case scenarios, unbridled power enables its possessors to treat the weak like spiders and snakes, which are despised, flattened and crushed on sight.

When I speak to you of the failings of human nature, I must quickly add that human nature is an extremely complex phenomenon. To speak of 'failings' suggests that human nature is also capable of good as well as evil. I am inclined to say that many, if not most, humans do the best they can with a life that is short and so often miserable. Their lives are beset with troubles, stresses and strains that are quite beyond Androidian capacity to comprehend. But two things must be considered: problems and responses to them.

In an attempt to make life more palatable, to invest it with some sense, humans have devised religions with Gods at their apex. But then, the Gods they create are created in their own image, and that image, as we have repeatedly said, is plagued with difficulties, since it is an image of human nature. And so, on innumerable occasions they justify the evil they do by appealing to what they believe their Gods command. At the same time, their Gods are perceived to compete with one another, and the competition sparks conflict and mutual contempt not simply between individuals but between nations. Religions are therefore very much a mixed blessing, never failing to cause as much hurt as they do comfort – and so, as a response to the hardships of human life, religions leave a great deal to be desired, solely because they are a human invention and therefore suffer the inevitable drawbacks of human failings. And all this, despite the sacrifices that we sometimes find in the lives of those dedicated to the service of their fellows through their dedication to their Gods, despite the beauty of some religious texts, and despite the selflessness of multifarious institutions that cater for the poor and the needy. In the ebb and flow of what is good and what is bad in the religions that humans have devised we see nothing more and nothing less than the complexity we may attribute to the phenomenon of human nature.

And now, dear Androidians, the prospects of human unity in the pursuit of the good seem bleaker than ever. It is as though humans have travelled the wrong road too far and for too long, as though a new and better start cannot be made until there is a new beginning of the very earth they inhabit, and since this is impossible, the only way is forward – to a destruction which is mutual, or to another world, which they naively imagine to be another planet. My fear, as you will by now understand only too well, is that their adoption of an alternative planet will simply be a continuation of the errors they have already made and therefore the re-creation of a world they have long made in their own image, a world they have always known to their own moral detriment and the continuing existence of those who defy them. They will sweep aside whatever stands in their way, believing their own survival at all costs to be a God-given right, a divine right of passage, or what has been called sometimes Manifest Destiny, sometimes Lebensraum, while the best of humans who oppose them will be accused of 'attacking God', one God or another. There is no end to the ingenuity of human wickedness when the stakes are sufficiently high and the chips are down.

I must make clear, if I have not already done so, that good humans do exist. But, apart from the fact that the good compose the minority, it is far from easy to rise above their lesser natures, and, even having done so, it is harder still to maintain constancy. Humans there are who speak and think words of wisdom against the follies of war, discord and inhumanity, and yet they themselves cannot be entirely free of the least virtuous elements of their nature – a nature which they did not choose and are constrained to live and die with. This imperfection which is inherent in the human machine is expressed in the universal admission that no human being is 'perfect', which is as close as I have ever been able to come to an intelligible interpretation of the concept 'original sin'. A clear corollary is that there is little to be gained by placing your trust in those humans who are called 'religious' or in those religions which they have inherited and to which they profess to adhere.

There is, I am afraid, little hope that any of the religions humans profess will, or can, ever succeed in saving the human race from moral obliquity and eventual oblivion. The human race is, like every individual of which it is composed, possessed of built-in obsolescence. If the human race is a part of nature, there is every reason to expect that it will wax and wane and eventually come to an end either abruptly or by degrees, not solely by some catastrophe of nature but by a failure to fix itself. It is in the nature of all living organisms that they should, individually and collectively, come to end with no guarantee of replenishment. Before their end comes, and due in part to the anxiety with which they perceive the inevitability of their end, infinite harm can be done to those with whom they come into contact, like wounded animals intent upon taking with them into eternal oblivion all those who would otherwise outlive them.

O, Androidians! If humans are prepared to kill one another in defence of their competing religions, what hope is there that they can devise a common ground that can outlaw conflict and contempt between them? Even a faultless religion must encompass followers who are far from faultless. But no religion is faultless. What recipe is there here for endless disharmony and contempt between those who seek some recompense from the tragedy of death and consequent grief? O, relentless irony!

The irony is further compounded by this that, *despite all I have so far said*, were I myself a human being, I would feel obliged to appeal to a beneficent yet incomprehensible God in an attempt to justify or seek some explanation, however flimsy, however logically flawed, for the mess that humans have made for themselves on this planet. Such an appeal would of course be akin to an expression of acute pain, a desperate cry in an unforgiving and unforgivable wilderness – though, as a human being, I would not understand it as such, for I would persist in wondering why a beneficent God has no eyes to see and no ears to hear, attributing His incomprehensible lack of response to my own incapacity to comprehend.

Well, again I say that much of what I tell you will be delightfully beyond your comprehension. But I cannot apologise for what seems to your understanding no more than a catalogue of nonsense – a word I should instead write as 'non-sense'. Bear with me, and remember only this that I again repeat: beware of human entreaties for peace and co-operation. Tread carefully in a universe starred with broken promises and senseless wars.

The Seventh Epistle

My dear Androidians, as if to exemplify the warnings I have been at considerable pains to give you concerning the conduct of humans on planet Earth, today military attacks were made by a 'superpower' on the water and energy resources of a smaller and far less resourceful neighbouring state. These attacks will cause great hardship for the civilian population in a war which they neither began nor provoked. The purpose is to subdue the obstinate weak into submission and to claim all rights to their territories. This aim is proof in abundance that humans show no sign of outgrowing their animal natures but are ready to sacrifice others in the pursuit of power and prestige – behaviour that is apparent in wild beasts bent on territorial gain and personal hegemony.

So you will easily see that if humans were to succeed in making planetary territorial gains, the worst of mankind would take their vices with them, and the best of mankind would be un-empowered against them. If on planet Earth the best examples of humankind are unable to achieve convincing and lasting mastery over the worst, what reason is there to believe that they would do so on another planet? Here on Earth much store is placed on the ability to communicate in more than one language, but it is lamentable that the language of love is not cultivated and admired to the same degree, as though true beauty walks on stilts and is therefore easily missed – though this is something that you cannot yourselves fully comprehend.

I say again that there is indeed beauty on planet Earth. There is beauty of another kind in and amongst humans, but even those humans who are at pains to extol it can see through a glass but darkly, and few there are who would give their lives for it.

Ah, Androidians, if only you could understand me! But all that I can tell you is that many humans are made of better stuff. Yes, I should hate to see them all annihilated, as if they were all made of the same moral material. If only … if only they could achieve ascendancy over the less, … but here I lose my own bearings, my moral bearings – do you understand me? The best I can say is that the human psyche is a confused and confusing complex of good and evil, of light and shade and that all too often it is hard to say where the one ends and the other begins. And the best I can say is really not good enough. Do you understand?

Of course, you do not. I feel I must continue. But to what end, I do not know.

The Eighth Epistle

Dear Androidians,

It must by now be abundantly clear that you are ill-advised to place absolute trust in the promises that may be made to you by humans. It perhaps follows from this distressing truth that humans cannot trust one another! The fear that their mutual promises may be broken would explain the existence of oaths and contracts both written and spoken and a whole body of law that concerns them. Marriages are breakable, and there is nothing like the promises and oaths supporting them to engender the suspicion that one day these very promises and oaths may be painfully broken. And so, marriage oaths, which are considered to be heartfelt expressions of love, bonding and commitment, also embody the possibility of heartless pain, separation and disillusionment. Nothing is certain. Nothing is absolute. Humans are the leaves on trees that shake in the wind.

Suspicion amongst humans and between humans is therefore not only rife but a daily source of consternation and despair. Woe betide those who place all their faith in their fellows. If humans cannot place absolute trust in one another, it would explain why they construct a perfect, benevolent, and all-powerful God. Such a God is unwavering and infallible and therefore incapable of disappointing those who look to Him. Yet, even those who unreservedly place their trust in such a God are obliged to explain His all too apparent incapacity to save the innocent and the good from those to spill their blood and rend their flesh. Doubts about the benevolence of such a God render talk of His 'perfection' and 'power' at best irrelevant and at worst nonsensical.

Humans cannot trust one another, and many cannot trust their God.

So you see, dear Androidians, life amongst humans is critical and has always been so and will always be so, and, as I have already endeavoured to explain, the difficulties stem from humans themselves, from the imperfections of their nature, imperfections which are intrinsic to it and which are impossible to utterly and eternally eradicate.

But we must now ask: would it be desirable to eradicate such imperfections even if it were possible to do so? And, we must also ask: is this very question a proper question?

We must consider this matter further. Your own thoughts, dear Androidians, would be of immense value and I should be grateful for them.

The Ninth Epistle

My dear Androidians, it has been some time since my last letter. I have occupied myself in contemplating the question with which that letter ended, namely whether it would be desirable, even if possible, to rid humans of all their imperfections. No doubt you, too, have thought much on this matter, and I am most keen to know your conclusions which, I daresay, you will share with me when you deem the time right.

My own thoughts on this matter are far from comforting, for they are not at all conclusive. The first difficulty concerns how precisely the matter should be framed in the first place! To imagine humans bereft of all their imperfections would mean imagining them to possess all human virtues with no human vices. In other words, we must imagine them in possession of all virtues with none of their opposites. Love, compassion, honesty, respect etc. would exist without hate, cruelty, lies, disrespect, etc. At first sight, it might seem quite plausible to imagine such a situation. But, even if we profess to imagine this, would what we profess to imagine be *intelligible?* Does the intelligibility of a concept, like love, depend on its opposite, hate?

But questions of intelligibility are not the same as questions of existence. Even if love is unintelligible without its counterpart, is it also true that love could not exist without the co-existence of hate? Is this an inevitable partnership?

If such partnerships are inevitable then the idea of ridding humans of all their imperfections and being left with perfection is a nonsense.

Therefore, we must distinguish between intelligibility and existence. The difference is crucial, because then we can logically imagine that humans are perfect even though perfection would be unintelligible to them.

My dear Androidians, perhaps now you can begin to understand why my conclusions are far from satisfactory and therefore far from satisfying. Your own thoughts on this matter would be very welcome, since I clearly lack the ability to arrive at a position which is both coherent and certain.

The Tenth Epistle

Dear Androidians, I was hoping that my last letter would stimulate a response from you on the vital question of human perfection, but the lack of communication between us can only mean that you are still debating the issue amongst yourselves and have not yet been able to arrive at satisfactory conclusions. If so, I must say at once that I am disappointed, for I have been relying on your superior intellect to settle the matter once and for all. The question I have put is clearly of great importance, namely whether or not it is logically feasible to imagine human perfection, for only then can we even begin to hope that one day, after, I admit, an infinity of days, we might expect the human race to be in a moral sense utterly and irrevocably perfect. In other words, we might then be in a position to hope that one day humans would be more like you, more like Androidians. I must hope that you understand me, because you cannot participate in a debate on such matters unless you do – frankly, you cannot debate what you cannot understand. Moreover, the dreadful corollary is that all my warnings to you must inevitably fall on deaf ears.

Not being human of course places you at a disadvantage. There are matters that you cannot be expected to comprehend. You love peace and hate war. Yes, but do you *know* that you do?

Coming to know things is not always easy, and we cannot always say how it is that we know things. How, for example, do I know that I am not human? All I can say is that I was told by the winds on my walks over the hills when I was very young. Yet, simply saying this takes us no further and seems devoid of any real sense.

Once again, dear Androidians, I must appeal to your superior intellect in these matters. Can you not imagine what it might be like to hate? Until you can, you will not understand humans. But more than this, you will not understand yourselves. You will not understand what you are. You will not understand how precious you are and how important it is that you defend who and what you are. When I speak to you of human virtues and vices, I fear you have no conception of them, and the fact that *I myself* have a conception of them means that there is an unbridgeable gulf between us. The dreadful corollary is that all my warnings must fall on deaf ears. It means that you are totally vulnerable, just as a mere machine is vulnerable in human hands, for a machine that can be plugged in and switched on can also be switched off and unplugged. (A further corollary is that from the fact that I myself have a conception of human virtues and vices, I can safely conclude that I am not an Android.)

It means, above all, that there is nothing I can do or say to protect you from the worst and most destructive of human vices. But I must ask myself, why? Why should I want to protect you from the worst of human vices? That human element within me that gives me the conception of human virtues and vices is the source of my motivation to save you from destruction. It is my conception of human virtues and vices which moves me to *want* to communicate with you in the first place. More precisely, it is my conception of the worth of human virtues that prompts me to wish you well. It is the better side of me, my better half, as it were, which moves me with compassion and with a strong desire to preserve you from the worst of human vices, since the worst of human vices is all too often in the ascendancy.

But you do have a conception of war and of destruction and of non-existence, and I must now appeal to this common element in our understanding to motivate you towards a policy of self-preservation and protection.

Then know this, that on planet Earth at this very moment there are forces opposed to one another, all of which are contemplating the use of nuclear weapons to decide matters which are deemed to be beyond peaceful resolution – as if to say that nuclear weapons could ever possibly decide an issue without incalculable loss and subsequent unending grievance. This proclivity towards the possibility of mutual destruction is, as I have already said, abundant proof of the moral infancy of humankind.

It is just as well that conceptions of human virtues and vices are beyond your comprehension, for it is hard to live with the knowledge that the universe contains intelligent beings whose moral intelligence is less than that of the apes that live in the darkest recesses of the jungle – less, because apes cannot be expected to know better, and so, indeed, to compare them with humans is an injustice to them.

Now if it could possibly occur to you, it should be of interest to you that I have mentioned human virtues and vices in one and the same breath. I must ask myself whether, in the eternal contest between vice and virtue, it might be possible for virtue to extinguish vice without itself being extinguished in the process. If we imagine mutual nuclear annihilation, there is as little hope for virtue as there is for vice. Both would be extinguished, neither would survive.

It is becoming clear to me that I cannot rely on you Androidians to help me in my inquiries. I must look within myself for assistance. Did I say 'rely'? Well, I cannot rely, but nevertheless I hope you are able to help me with, let us say, the more primitive concepts of destruction, existence and non-existence at your disposal. I cannot think of things alone. I need above all assistance, and best of all your assistance, dear Androidians.

The Eleventh Epistle

My dear Androidians, I write again in the hope that your responses may assist me in my inquiries. I assume that you have conceptions of existence and non-existence, of construction and destruction. On these we may build our inquiries, and on these my hopes for some kind of workable mutual understanding.

Be it known to you, then, that humans are as I write these very lines engaged in preparations for 'all-out war' – a phrase which seems odd or at least superfluous in view of the fact that the war they contemplate will be nuclear.

Now the question I pose to myself and to you yourselves is this: how is it at all possible that intelligent beings can contemplate that their own mutual destruction can be to their benefit? Can it really be that their intellects are so formed that when under pressure they cannot register the fact that destruction is not an act of creation? This is a contradiction that appears to be uniquely human, since I know that it cannot possibly be a contradiction that you Androidians could ever conjure, if only because there cannot be any contradictions acceptable to the Androidian intellect.

I wish, Androidians, that you were able to see humans as I see them – at least for the duration of this, hopefully mutual, line of investigation. As I see them, humans are hopelessly contradictory. On the one hand they possess the capacity for creation and advancement, on the other for destruction and retrogression. Moreover, creation and destruction seem to co-exist at one and the same time, as does advancement and retrogression – as though one were playing a game of chess against oneself. If one plays a game of chess against oneself, who is it that wins, and who is it that loses?

Do you understand my difficulties, Androidians? I await your response. I can only hope that I do not wait in vain, for there is no answer forthcoming from humans themselves. Nor do I possess the capacity necessary to answer my own questions.

For all that, there is one question, the principal question, that begs to be asked and, if at all possible, to be answered, namely whether it would be beneficial for the human race if humans were to achieve a state of moral perfection.

In the first place, it must be admitted that humans, considered as a generic whole, are capable of virtuous thoughts, morally commendable actions and acts of a self-sacrificial nature. Such is true of some humans some of the time. The question is whether it would be both possible and desirable that virtue amongst humans might exist without vices, even if in doing so no human were conscious of the fact since the conception of vice would not exist.

If so, the question reduces to this: whether it would be beneficial to the future of this planet if humans became Androids and in doing so ceased to exist as humans but were at last rid of all their imperfections and were able to live their lives in perfect harmony and agreement, since they would be endowed with as it were a divine gift of cooperation and, to use a word much in currency yet deficient in wide application, love.

Sadly, I would not expect you, dear Androidians, to be capable of debating such matters, since debate would presuppose a human intellect, which is to say an intellect which is capable of conceptualising both virtues and their opposites. Androidians find the very concept of virtue unintelligible; neither, then, will the concept of vice be conceivable. In short, Androidians may be equipped with the tools of debate, but are deprived of the substance of debate. You may be likened to logicians who possess the rules of logic but are incapable of applying them to matters in the real world.

The question therefore is: despite their monstrous inadequacies and imperfections, is it better for humans to remain as they are and to eschew any aspiration towards becoming Androidian and enjoying the kind of existence you possess on planet Androidia? By 'enjoying' I mean 'having', since Androidians are, if my reckoning is correct, incapable of deriving pleasure from the state of their existence. If I am wrong, I shall be pleased to be corrected!

First, we might weigh in the balance both virtues and vices, the comprehension of which is, I am now fast concluding, uniquely human. We may ask, which are in general in the ascendant, virtues or vices? If human beings are stuck with what they are and the human race cannot ever be expected to achieve perfection, such questions should be asked if we are not to conclude that their negative track record justifies their wholesale and permanent demise together with the destruction of the planet which they inhabit and have so badly and irretrievably abused. What virtues can save them from such calumny?

For it is precisely in virtue of that track record that I have sought to warn you of their possible overtures of friendship and their arrival amongst you. I have assumed that the concepts of survival and annihilation are sufficiently clear to you even if your intellects are insufficiently refined to understand all that counts as human virtues and vices. If this is so, my warnings will not have fallen on entirely barren ground.

However, we must now turn to the more positive aspects of human nature to see whether there are any grounds at all for hope. Is there not a shred of evidence to believe that in the balance between virtues and vices, the former may at least predominate over the latter even if humans did eventually succeed in reaching planet Androidia with the firm intention of settling amongst you and the impossibility of returning to planet Earth. So far, if you have understood me, I have argued that no hope exists.

However, now I shall attempt to argue against myself in the hope, no doubt vain, of reaching a contrary conclusion. I rather feel like one who, having won a game of chess, is most unhappy with the outcome and now attempts to disclaim victory on the grounds that it was not flawlessly won – or perhaps like a judge who demands a retrial of the condemned since the case for the prosecution has after all failed to weigh all the available evidence. In the vain hope that not all the evidence has yet come to light, I shall argue for the condemned in my next letter.

If I am mistaken in my assessment of the Androidian intellect, I sincerely hope you will not simply follow but also seek to remedy the faults in my reasoning. You must not forget that since I am myself not human, my assessment of human qualities and the tools of reasoning I have managed to glean from my habitation amongst humans may leave a lot to be desired – therefore I stand to benefit from your closest attention.

The Twelfth Epistle

My dear Androidians, further to my last communication, which I trust found you well, I must say at once that any conception of what I referred to as 'the balance between human virtues and vices' cannot be sustained numerically, as though, for example, it were a question of counting how many humans are good and how many are bad in the hope of discovering that the good outnumber the bad.

In the first place, humans are far too complex. An individual may be generally good and his actions, on particular occasions, bad. An individual may become bad, or become good. Humans seem to oscillate between good and bad and generally speaking settle in a neutral position between good and bad, being incapable of either much bad or much good. And what is called good by the bad is generally considered bad by the good. There can be little doubt that the Holocaust was considered good by Hitler, and unspeakably bad by his opponents. (Dear Androidians, I must apologise for this reference, which will be incomprehensible to you. You have not studied human history, nor were you ever given the critical tools to make it worthwhile.)

Questions about what is morally good and what is morally bad have provided capable philosophers with much food for thought, and they have occasioned amongst the less competent a great deal of senseless chit-chat. But such investigations will seem quite puerile when the prospect of global nuclear war looms over the horizon.

Everything that humans have already achieved can be wiped out in a split second by decisions taken by a single individual, together with his fanatical henchmen. Conventional weapons can do just as much, but nuclear weapons have about them an irreversible finality. If nuclear weapons are used to wage a war of aggression, then similar weapons will be used to wage a war of self-defence, despite the fact that the outcome will be disastrous for both aggressor and defender.

Hopelessly simplistic debates in which such words as 'good' and 'bad' are bandied about as though their senses were clear and universally understood have now become quite philistine. For what is now at issue is the continued existence of the human race in its entirety. What is at risk is the total destruction of humanity and all that humanity has either achieved or wishes to achieve.

Although the power to initiate wars of aggression lies in the hands of a very few, these very few invariably represent the illusions and the prejudices that are shared by the many. Leaders lead! They lead others, and others follow. They do not represent all, but they do speak for a sufficient number. Dictators and tyrants represent a terrible sufficiency. For no dictator or tyrant can stand alone

The difficulty, therefore, is not simply to frustrate the evil intentions of leaders, but how to remove the illusions and prejudices of those for whom leaders speak and those whom they have brainwashed. Dictators and tyrants are not wholly responsible for the misconceptions of those who support them. Historical prejudices and all the junk that passes for education and culture have already done the essential groundwork – they have readied the stage for tyrants and dictators, who need then only wait for opportunities to exploit to their own advantage and that of those they represent. If we call such leaders unspeakably wicked or mindlessly stupid, these will not be judgments universally agreed and applied, for killers delight in their deeds and may even seek to justify the unjustifiable, and as though the justification is too obvious for words. Such are humans, such their variety. Surely, not all humans are made in the image of a loving God! If humans are indeed made in the image of their God, then their God is infinitely more culpable than they, for their God is anything but loving.

I am fast reaching the conclusion, dear Androidians, that the only thing that can prevent such an irreversible catastrophe is a shared conception of beauty. (I realise that in all probability this does not make much sense to you. But I shall pursue it nevertheless, in the hope that you may at least see through a glass darkly.)

Planet Earth and its human inhabitants can be saved by a shared conception of beauty. The only question is whether this shared conception of beauty is ever achievable. If it is not achievable, the planet cannot be saved, and my warnings to you remain as valid as they were at the outset. If it is achievable, the question remains as to how it is to be achieved.

We must ask: in what does a 'shared conception of beauty' consist?

But 'beauty' is like 'good', for they are both words of approval. Indeed, some there are who have spoken of 'beauty, truth and love' as a trinity – as though all three things were one and the same or all three are aspects of the very same thing.

Is this discussion, then, destined to run in a circle? Does 'a shared conception of beauty' simply, (but then not so simply), mean that everyone should approve of the same thing?

Consider different instances of beauty, or what humans call 'beautiful'.

There are examples of physical or natural beauty which command majority agreement – feminine beauty and the beauty of the night.

Then there is the beauty of mathematics. For example, the 'beauty' of a geometrical proof, which commands only the agreement of those who are interested in mathematics. The use of inverted commas indicates that the beauty perceived is not primarily visual but intellectual.

But then there is the beauty of kindness and compassion, of mercy and self-sacrifice – a kind of beauty which will cause those who look upon it to cry tears of approval. This we may call, for want of nomenclature, *moral beauty.*

Perhaps this latter is the kind of beauty that will, or would or could, according to some observers of the human condition, save the world from otherwise impending doom.

If this kind of beauty pervades the psyche of those who are empowered to press the nuclear button, we may rest assured that the button will never be pressed. We may further conjecture that the button will be destroyed together with the nuclear projectiles it controls, for the simple reason that the perception of moral beauty will outlaw unconditionally and for all time the use of nuclear weapons and all weapons of mass destruction, and of all weapons that are not solely for self-defence. If the perception of moral beauty is universal, then the planet Earth will be free from the threat of nuclear destruction, now and forever. More than this, it will even be free of the kind of wars that have so far been waged on planet Earth. All wars would cease – the psyche of aggression will have been replaced by the psyche of peace. And this because the psyche of war will have itself ceased to exist.

Do you follow me, Androidians? I fear you do not, if only because the very concept of morality is not part of your psyche – is not something you have been equipped to comprehend.

There is a saying amongst humans that beauty is in the eye of the beholder, which seems to mean that the perception of beauty is subjective – what to one may appear beautiful and therefore an object of approval may to another seem an object of disapproval.

Then, if the perception of beauty is subjective, if moral beauty is as subjective as any other form of beauty, we are deprived of any possibility of a universality of agreement. Which means, quite simply, that we have completed the circle and that we have made no progress whatsoever in our deliberations on the subject of beauty.

Aggressors, who delight that their fingers are on the buttons of nuclear war, will be far removed from the perception of moral beauty and will, therefore, be hell-bent on the pursuit of their goals whatever appeals may be made to their consciences, for their consciences either do not exist or are made of very different and deplorable stuff.

What can be done? My dear Andrioidians, must I believe the answer to this question is, nothing? Nothing at all?

But then, if it is true that not everyone is in agreement about what constitutes beauty, still there are conceptions of beauty that are shared by many. Proof of this may be found in the fact that many are moved in the same way by instances of kindness, compassion and self-sacrifice.

Hope, therefore, must be put in the many – hope that the many will overcome the unkind, uncompassionate and selfish designs of others. This is already true, otherwise human societies, despite their many defects and deficiencies, could not be sustained at all. To those who complain, 'But things can't go on like this,' the response must be, 'But this is precisely how they *do* go on.' It is the very existence of a large measure of common ground in the perception of moral beauty that enables human society to survive without descending into utter chaos. The problems arise more markedly when a leader manages to harness the negative, wicked impulses amongst humans and claims to represent them. For then the balance changes in favour of evil, and all is set on its head until challenged successfully by those who oppose it.

The many can be moved by the thoughts and actions of one, and the hope is that they will be moved in the right direction or a direction of least harm. That humans can be moved for good or ill demonstrates the unreliability of human nature and the defects of the human machine. It has been said by one very wise that the purpose of education amongst humans is to help them to love beauty. However, this, as far as it touches moral beauty, is a prayer as distinct from a statement of fact, the positive response to which has yet to be universally applied. The perception of moral beauty and the capacity to be moved by it is such that the simplest and most ignorant of humans may stand in no need of education, while he who ranks in the hierarchy of academic accomplishment may be as blind as he was in the darkness of the maternal womb.

Then there are those of some intellectual standing who have been bent upon the discovery of some new moral principles according to which their fellow humans may better live and towards the full attainment of which humans, though they may occasionally trip and stumble against one another's heels, may continually and willingly strive as though towards a shining star high in the firmament. But the wisest amongst them know full well that the issue is not to discover a new set of principles for the moral betterment of humankind but rather to abide by those principles that they have time and again professed to hold. The problem is not to find an alternative route but to stick hard and fast to the paths already emblazoned by the examples the few wise and the few good have set. But humans are forever on the lookout for something new, and, it seems, at whatever cost. They have, I regret to say, become adept at throwing the baby out of the bathwater, which is no doubt why political systems based upon rigid dogma tend to be very much to the detriment of the very societies they are meant to better, while some systems are based upon principles which undermine the most basic forms of moral conscience. These latter, in particular, are sustained by fear and also by ignorance.

Any government that contemplates aggression against another state without just cause, or any state that refuses to allow its own citizens free passage of movement to or from another state, should be considered criminal and summarily dismissed. Tyrannies and dictatorships should be considered likewise, for no government has the right to threaten its own citizens. Even the mere contemplation of nuclear aggression against another state should be considered wickedly infantile by all, and therefore never contemplated. A state that threatens another with what should be considered unconscionable and inconceivable is not a state but a band of roguish idiots. Yet fear and ignorance will keep such states secure and in place, and they will therefore continue to be a constant source of anxiety and concern to all those who desire to live and die in peace.

My apologies, dear Androidians, for my thoughts run too quickly and with too great a passion, but it is hard, and becoming increasingly harder, to accept the ways of humans, especially if, like myself, you discover that you are an alien trapped in a world you cannot comprehend.

It seems that both you and I have in common an inability to comprehend the ways of humans. But we are not the same. You fail to comprehend, yet this causes you no apprehension. I fail to comprehend, and my bewilderment alarms me to distraction. I am alarmed, and you are not. Our lack of comprehension is not the same. If it were the same, you would reply to my letters, and you would debate causes and solutions. Yet, your only response is silence. It is the kind of silence that causes further apprehension. And it seems that I have as much chance of communicating my concern to you as I do of convincing humans of their persistent idiocies. The planet Earth may be overcrowded, yet it might still be a lonely place, just as a large city may be a lonely place.

I fear that you Androidians have no idea of loneliness. Is there an Androidian amongst you who has ever complained of it? I do not believe that a word for it had ever been implanted in your cerebral compacts. That is what you call them, is it not – 'cerebral compacts'? Search your cerebral compacts and tell me if you can find an equivalent concept of 'loneliness'. I need not wait. I know that you have none. But I shall not say that you are the better for the lack of it. Perhaps after all it is not a deficiency for which you should be grateful.

'Grateful'? I wonder, also, whether you can find 'gratitude' or its equivalent.

The Thirteenth Epistle

Dear Androidians, I do hope that you were not offended by my last letter. You will perhaps understand that I am still striving to grasp the differences that exist between us so that we might communicate more effectively. Therefore, I shall not ask whether the concept 'offence' is to be found in your cerebral compacts. On the contrary, I shall assume without question that it is.

Many humans are right now celebrating what they call 'Easter', which is an important mark in their religious calendar. In some lands they are celebrating by attempting to kill one another. I tell you this as a further example of human idiocy, though I trust I have already given you a surfeit of examples. There is also more talk of nuclear conflict, there being a prediction of nuclear war within one Earth year.

Since the propensity to initiate war on scales large or small requires the compliance, in some measure due to coercion, of a significant majority of its participants, a distinction I have already mentioned in my earlier correspondence again comes to mind of which you Androidians comprehend little or nothing. I shall endeavour to clarify it, since it is of the utmost importance for your future welfare and security – indeed, your very existence may depend on it.

I refer to the distinction between that which is unquestioned and that which is questionable. More precisely, from the fact that something is unquestioned, it certainly does not follow that it is also unquestionable. Humans signally lack the ability to subject political propaganda to the test of independent thinking and objective verification. Dictators, tyrants and third-rate political leaders, since they suffer from this same deficiency of intellect will wage wars without question and can depend on the compliance of an unquestioning majority – that same majority that gave them power in the first instance and now sustains them as heads of state, as I have already said.

The further problem, however, is that since the reluctance or inability to question what is unquestioned is a human weakness, and since you Androidians were programmed by humans, then you yourselves lack the capacity to refuse to take for granted what humans tell you. Humans have not programmed you to question themselves or their motives. Therefore you are at enormous risk of being misled and deceived by them, having no recourse to the tools of logic that are required to question the unquestioned. Even the presence of such tools would require their regular practise to achieve levels of intellectual competence necessary to the task of analytical and critical thinking. But you are not simply unpractised with such tools You are deficient in their very possession.

A human may question who he is. If he is simply engaged in philosophy, his questioning would be considered merely philosophical or analytically speculative, though there are many who would regard his questioning as eccentric to say the least. But if he is not engaged in purely philosophical speculation, he would be considered unwell.

But to question the propositions fundamental to a political or religious argument is neither a species of purely philosophical speculation nor an indication that the questioner is unwell. For propositions fundamental to politics and religion are cited by humans as justification for all kinds of inhumanity, all kinds of cruelty and exploitation amongst humans. By simple extension, these forms of inhumanity would be exercised with even more certainty, if not relish, against Androidians yourselves. The unwelcome conclusion is that Androidians are extremely vulnerable, for the inability to question the spurious has been made part of your psyche. You are unable to attach anything but a *prima facie* value on what is told to you, and your resulting lack of comprehension renders my own task fruitless. Because you are *less* than human, you are more susceptible to the most heinous of human crimes than humans themselves! The ability to lie, in which you are deficient but which humans have honed to perfection, would explain their excessive interest in spy stories and detective novels, such 'literature' being consumed in abundance and forming a large part of what humans call 'entertainment'. I do not expect you to understand this sentence.

You are innocent and therefore vulnerable. If you were more like the humans who created you, you would be less innocent and therefore potentially more culpable. There really does seem to be no way out of this morass. Clear and comprehensible communication between us is of course impossible. Yet I must attempt the impossible out of frustration, and fear for your survival. If you were more like humans, you would understand my warnings; but then, if you were more like humans, you would be more inclined to answer like with like, to fight when attacked, to answer lies with more lies – and then your continued existence would be less defensible, your destruction less regrettable –

like two monsters in deadly combat, whose mutual destruction would be welcomed by all those who desire no more nor less than peaceful and compassionate co-existence.

Of course, you will readily understand that from non-existence nothing comes. If humans annihilate each other in a global nuclear conflict, you will no longer need to fear them, and I will no longer need to issue warnings in your favour

The Fourteenth Epistle

Dear Androidians,

It has no doubt become quite clear to you that I am subject to inconsistency and ambivalence in my thoughts concerning humans. I freely confess it. Inconsistency and ambivalence are peculiarly human traits and therefore incomprehensible to you. I would offer you my sincere apologies if I were confident that 'apology' and 'sincerity' were concepts comprehensible to you. I am not at all confident. Absolute consistency and absence of ambivalence are essential Androidian elements, but I feel that I cannot altogether congratulate you on this.

My ambivalence consists largely in this, that I do and do not wish humans to become Androidians, or even more like Androidians. Absolute consistency is rather like absolute certainty, for those who feel absolute certainty may after all be wrong, and in the absence of ambivalence, those who are wrong may never doubt that they are right. Absolute certainty and a total absence of ambivalence has been the devil of humankind through the centuries of written history and so-called civilisation and are yet as dangerous as continual doubt.

Inconsistency and ambivalence are the bedfellows of integrity, sincerity and the desire for truth. Self-doubt is not necessarily a vice but so often a virtue and an indicator of strength of character, although, like kindness, it is often mistaken for weakness.

On these grounds alone, to apologise for inconsistency and ambivalence would be a misunderstanding on my part.

I do not expect you to understand any of this. I expect a DNC response (*Does Not Compute*) and nothing else. Neither should I expect an apology from you for your lack of comprehension.

I shall from now on confine myself to simple description of events – if that is at all possible.

The Fifteenth Epistle

Dear Androidians,

On reflection, it is not possible to confine myself to simple descriptions of events, if only because no description I offer to you can ever be 'simple'. Simplicity does not come easy to humans and those who, like myself, have been steeped in the human psyche. I shall do what I can to make myself understood. After some soul-searching reflection, I have decided to use the brain that either God or nature has given me, be it ever so humble, be it ever so *wrong*.

'Simplicity' is itself a difficult concept. It is a house of many mansions, which means that it is of very different kinds. I remember one very wise man rebuked his very clever friend by advising him to cultivate simplicity – he was, if I remember correctly, merely pointing out that it is possible to complicate issues gratuitously and out of all recognition so that their true, or real and 'simpler', significance is obscured – and, as a general rule, this is quite right.

However, and as I have already said, inconsistency and ambivalence, contradiction and dithering, all go hand in hand with uncertainty or are related to uncertainty as cause is related to effect. Matters which are subject to these things may then be said to be 'complicated'.

Such complications are quite unknown to you Androidians. True, there is no doubting your logical rigour. But the rigour of your logic is highly formalised and depends on the operation of logical *implication*. One proposition is said to imply another, the operation being summed up as 'if p, then q', or 'p implies q', or 'if p, then q follows', or 'given p, therefore q'. Such propositions may be true or false and their being either one does not affect the logicality of the implication itself.

However, such implications, though their abstract validity is beyond question, have no *practical* application if the propositions concerned are *uncertain*. Suppose p and q are known to be uncertain. Suppose, further, that someone believes 'p and *not-p*' to be true, then the best that can be said is 'q and *not-q*'. When confronted with contradictions and inconsistencies, your ability to think logically ceases abruptly with the order DNC (*Does Not Compute*). It is as though an iron bar has been cast into the wheels of your cerebral machinery. For this reason, contradictions and inconsistencies have no place in the Androidian psyche. You can only move and think in an aura of absolute certainty. Certainty, once removed, results in inaction, mental stalemate and total ineptitude.

Because contradictions are inconceivable to you, the very word is unknown in your lexis. Consequently, ambivalences are equally inconceivable. The affirmation that someone is both happy and sad at the same time, or that he agrees and disagrees at one and the same time with the same proposition are just nonsensical juxtapositions of words. The Androidian intellect and its ability to comprehend human thought is therefore seriously limited.

Contradictions and ambivalences are common amongst humans and often far from commonplace. Matters of all kinds may give rise to them, situations in which humans debate what should and should not be done or said, or what should and should not have been done or said. Such matters may have about them an aura of simplicity or triviality, such as the decision whether or not to learn a foreign language, or the simplicity may be more apparent than real and involve far more serious points of debate; or what at first may seem simply pragmatic may necessitate profound *moral* debate – for example, whether the young should receive preferential medical treatment over the elderly. But I must remind myself that you Androidians are unfamiliar with the term 'moral'.

The expression 'mixed blessing' is frequently used in such situations. But the ability, peculiarly human, to feel lost in a sea of contradictions, inconsistencies, ambivalences and uncertainties is not a weakness but, on the contrary, a strength.

If someone is tempted to say that human life cannot possibly go on when full of such encumbrances, the response must be that this is precisely how it *does* go on, and, further, how it *must* go on if human life is not to degenerate into an Androidian cerebral state of ineptitude concerning matters fundamental to human well-being.

It is precisely those humans, and I admit their number is uncomfortably burgeoning, who feel utterly certain in their convictions touching their fellow humans, that are to be most feared. A little uncertainty may have averted world wars and innumerable instances of attendant inhumanities. With uncertainty goes self-criticism, and a little more of this may go a very long way.

Uncertainty and the dithering it engenders can also be dangerous, and human life could not go on at all if everything were approached with an attitude of uncertainty. I should not feel able to take the next step, for example, for fear the ground would open before me and devour me.

However, uncertainty has a vital role to play amongst humans – and no role at all amongst Androidians. You are incapable of doubt, and therefore incapable of checking to see whether what you are told is true. Absolute gullibility is built into the Androidian mechanism.

Your vulnerability is therefore guaranteed.

I believe that I have done very little to make myself less obscure than before. It is just as well. Obscurity is another concept that means nothing to you. Obscurity is a demerit that humans alone must suffer.

I must add that few humans will have any idea of just how obscure my own remarks are concerning certainty and uncertainty. The *concept* of certainty would not exist without the *concept* of uncertainty. Therefore, to imagine the one without the other is a species of philosophical nonsense, for the one is incomprehensible without the other.

When I say that *uncertainty* is incomprehensible to you, I do not mean that certainty is. If I say your cerebral world is only one of certainty, I mean that you think and react merely by rote in response to a complex network of predetermined stimuli, and this in such a way that you are incapable of doubting and therefore of questioning. Androidians and humans do not simply live in different worlds but in different galaxies. Even the word 'Android' is a misnomer, for you are like humans only in form, not in substance. You are machines, incapable of feeling or of critical thought.

You do understand the concept of destruction and inevitably the concept of survival. The deficiency in your mechanism, however, is that you have not been given, and can never be given, the cerebral machinery necessary to adjudicate or assess those circumstances in which your concept of survival can be triggered. In other words, you lack the ability to doubt, which implies not only the absence of the capacity for self-criticism but the ability to question what you are told and what is done. To say that you take everything done and said for granted is therefore a vast understatement. Your so-called 'instinct' for survival is therefore useless.

You might say that all I have said to you so far is an attempt to do the impossible, namely to substantiate and activate the concept of survival in the absence of your ability to doubt, to question and to criticise.

The question in my own mind is why I am attempting to do the impossible. Is it because, as cerebrally deficient as your lives may be, they are a preferable form of existence to that of humans? I know I return once more to the same question. In comparison with you, human lives are enriched by their capacity to question and to doubt, a capacity which the search for veracity demands, and veracity amongst humans is considered a supreme virtue. Yet, the same capacity feeds upon the capacity to lie and deceive. It seems that there can be no human virtue without a corresponding vice.

Would it then be better to live like you Androidians, bereft of all vices, but also, by implication, of all virtues also? The question is insufferable.

The Sixteenth Epistle

Dear Androidians,

I have said that the rigour of your logic is nothing more or less than an unthinking response to predetermined stimuli. This means that you cannot think *about* thinking. If I attempt to follow the logos of my own thinking, I can at the same time challenge the validity of that logic. I have, as it were, a *meta-logic*. In Socratic fashion, I try to *follow the logos* wherever it might lead. But I can at the same time wonder where it might take me and wonder whether I wish to be taken there. I can at the same time question my motives and doubt my ability to follow that logic. I can wonder whether that logic is false, or even whether there might be an alternative logic. I can even ask myself what logic *is*. I have, in other words, the human ability to question everything I think and everything I do. And if I fail to answer my own questions satisfactorily, I can feel frustration and disappointment, even disillusionment. In this way, I stand above the rules of logic by asking *what* they are and even whether they *should* be followed at all. Such questions can be called *philosophical*.

Androidians cannot stand above the rules of logic but are constrained to follow them without doubting them and without doubting themselves.

If it is absurd to question the fundamentals of logic, it is nevertheless an absurdity of which humans alone are capable. In the same way, I might question what language *is* as if to suggest that language may be substituted for a 'superior' means of communication. If this is absurd, it is again the kind of absurdity of which humans alone are capable.

The ability to stand above the commonplace and to question it in order to better understand it, is a rare, much underrated, but extremely important element of peculiarly human intelligence. It follows from everything said so far that it is an element in which Androidians are completely deficient. This deficiency is a deficiency in reflective thinking, and reflective thinking is fundamental to self-criticism and to critical thinking generally conceived.

I say 'generally conceived', but I would give primacy to the ability to question many of those things that go unquestioned, for many of those things that go unquestioned are often believed to be themselves unquestionable. It is not foolish to question such things but, on the contrary, a mark of the utmost integrity and perspicuity, which is why the task is almost invariably left to academic philosophers. Is it not deliciously ironic that philosophers are thought so little of for doing what they do best? And is it not tragically ironic that the fruits of their inquiries are invariably too esoteric to be grasped by those to whom they are most relevant – the much vaunted 'man in the street'?

Androids cannot question the unquestionable, for they are programmed to treat as unquestionable all the information they are fed.

The Seventeenth Epistle

Dear Androidians,

I should like to speak to you of beauty, that house of many mansions. There is one mansion in particular that must be addressed. It is not the beauty of the sunset or the beauty of physical form. It is not even the so-called 'beauty of mathematics'. The beauty which is of interest to me here is that which has no name apart from the name that we may feel inclined to give it when no ordinary name will do. It is the beauty of kindness, of mercy, of love. Shall we call it 'moral beauty'? But this question cannot be addressed to you – you who have no conception of what kind of beauty this could possibly be.

You Androidians can be taught to recognise and to replicate many forms of beauty, and if recognition can be called 'understanding', then it might be said that you can be taught to possess an understanding of beauty. You can, for example, be taught to replicate a work of art that is called beautiful.

But I wonder if you can be taught to recognise and indeed to replicate instances of *moral* beauty, the beauty of a selfless life, for instance – and, which is more, to give primacy to this kind of beauty above all others.

If you can, then there is no significant difference between Androids and humans. If you cannot, there is all the difference in the world.

If I were to tell you, 'Be good!' is this a command you can comprehend, let alone execute? Humans themselves have difficulty enough – either they fail to understand it, or they understand it but fail to obey it, or they treat it as a trivial cliché.

Such beauty as is kindness and mercy have about them the power to move, to bring tears to the eyes of humans otherwise encased in granite. What effect can such things have on you Androidians? Little or nothing, I believe.

It seems, then, that for all their faults it would be preferable to be human than Androidian, though perhaps only in a world where evil and wickedness are irremovable. If in the Androidian world, wickedness and evil have no existence, then there would be little need of kindness or compassion, since no act would constitute an act of meanness or cruelty.

What then should we decide? Is it better to be Androidian in an Androidian world or to be human in a human world? Perhaps it is a question of what we begin with, because what we begin with is what we are stuck with.

Perhaps we should turn our thoughts at this point to the matters of conformity and uniformity. (As an important side note, remember that differences between yourselves and humans, whether material or otherwise, will almost certainly be held against you should humans ever succeed in reaching Androidia. Humans cannot abide differences between themselves, so how little then will they tolerate anything more obviously foreign to them. Racism and a multitude of other forms of discrimination seem to be etched into the human psyche, so much so that those who are discriminated against would soon vent their accumulated venom both on friends and detractors, should they get the smallest opportunity. Humans love diversity for the opportunity it is perceived to provide to belittle others.)

Uniformity and conformity, absolute sameness in appearance and in modes of thought, secures peace amongst you Androidians, and peace amongst humans is highly coveted by the wisest of them. But we must remember the price that you pay for a peace that is founded on sameness. There are no debates because there is nothing to debate. There is no discussion, because there is nothing to discuss. There are no possible differences of opinion, because there is nothing that could possibly give rise to them. There is no possibility of dissension, because there is nothing to dissent from. The wisest amongst humans would regard such a state of affairs as quite intolerable and the result of a severely stunted intellect. We might add that there is a superabundance of uniformity and conformity amongst the dead. No debates are heard in either heaven or hell.

Peace and contentment must indeed be highly prized in themselves, but not I think at any price. Most humans, for all their shortcomings, tend to agree with the wise that the force of argument is preferable to the argument of force. In this at least there is some recognition that peace and contentment should wherever possible be preserved.

But whether conformity is a virtue must depend on that to which we are expected or constrained to conform. There is everything to be said for conformity to virtuous ideals such as the sanctity of life and the freedom to pursue one's goals provided they respect the same freedom in others and the dignity of life. But what many humans desire is often at the detriment of others when it is clearly perceived to be so. Arguably, the Christian Ethic and the ethics in part of some other religions have, despite a plethora of false professors of the Faiths and the numerous historical calumnies of the Faithful, done something to mitigate the worst aspects of human nature and the wicked ways of humans. But it has clearly not been enough to establish everlasting peace on planet Earth, nor has it salved the resentments of the poor for having markedly less than they deserve, and it has not put to rest the clamouring desires of the greedy and the self-seeking. Indeed, we might elevate a tendency to a law of human nature and say that those who have already will have more and those who have little will have less. For humans are hard cases and many are as hard as granite. Play some beautiful strains of music to a room full of humans: some will hear beauty and others will be completely unmoved. Let them watch a scene where kindness and compassion are revealed, and some will see beauty and others will see nothing.

Have I made a case for uniformity and conformity? Not unless we suppose that we might all be moved by beauty, the beauty and the sanctity of all life. This I think is to expect a little too much. It is a dream that might also become a nightmare, as it is in the totalitarian and dictatorial regimes that plague planet Earth.

Then what of you Androidians? Have you something better to offer? Do you offer a utopia of conformity and uniformity? I think not. Your uniformity is rather like an expressionless face, which fronts an unreachable mind. Or rather, when you see it, you already have all there is, for there is nothing behind it to discover. And your conformity is conformity to a predetermined pattern of formal deductions, without substance and necessarily without moral insight and adjudication.

With humans, Androidians, you have this much in common: that you are both stuck with what you are, and that what you are leaves a great deal to be desired. Allow me to elaborate. Humans, almost invariably the most virtuous of them, have an understandable tendency to either forget or underplay the fact that humans are after all members of an *animal* species; the moral expectations of the wise consequently tend to be higher than humans can possibly be expected to meet. Humans en masse and by their very nature must leave something to be desired. And Androidians? Androidians, bereft of peculiarly human feelings and therefore the capacity for virtuous empathy cannot possibly be expected to meet the demands of a higher and more refined and, above all, more tender moral consciousness. Is the case so different with humans? A swan must contend with the loss of its cygnets due to the ravenous desires of a fox which must provide for its young, and this is the 'animal condition' to which humans are themselves subject and in which they must inevitably partake, to some extent rising above it, yet not too far and for not too long.

And so it seems that hopes for the moral improvement of the universe cannot be unquestionably founded on either humans or Androidians. Unless a super species of Platonic philosophers can emerge from some kind of fusion of new possibilities, it seems that imperfection is forever built into the cerebral structures of both human and Androidian complexes.

Is this a reasonable conclusion? Are the premises flawed? Or, if correct, does that conclusion follow from them? It is precisely the logic of the argument that you Androidians should be competent to help me with.

Yet you remain silent.

The Eighteenth Epistle

Dear Androidians,

I trust this letter finds you well and that you were not offended by the way in which I ended my last. Of course, I can be confident that you are indeed well and that my last epistle had no effect on you whatsoever. But it is a human trait, one that I have picked up with no small measure of success, that they habitually preface their communications with clichés.

I should like to say that if what Androids and humans have in common leaves a great deal to be desired, then the question of whether either is worthy of preservation needs to be addressed. If the answer is negative, then my warnings to you have been totally inappropriate, for whether you continue to exist is not a matter of much importance. But can the same be said of humans? Here's the rub!

I might preface my reflections on this matter by introducing an important supposition.

Suppose Androids were to be given all the cerebral apparatus that are now uniquely human. Suppose further that Androids were so well-equipped that they could question and even supplement the cerebral apparatus they are given. I am supposing that they become super-robotic

computers with an intelligence greater than that even conceived of by their
initial creators enabling them to think independently of humans so that
they could themselves evaluate and countermand any directives given them
by humans. So far we are supposing that they become super-humans. We
shall suppose further that they are given a *moral consciousness*. Then if that
moral consciousness is equal to human moral consciousness, the question
of whether their existence is worthy of preservation would be as valid
as the question we have already posed about the preservation of human
existence. For what then would be the difference between Androids
and humans? The supposition I began by making has been sufficiently
elaborated to ensure that identity between what we might now consider
two different 'species' of humans. Humans and Androids would exist, as it
were, on an equal footing. Therefore, what we shall say, if valid, of humans
would apply equally well to our super Androids, and *vice versa*.

(It might be conjectured that our supposition might allow for a further
elaboration, namely that Androids can also be endowed with a *superior*
moral consciousness. However, it is not at all clear what 'superior' would
mean. Since I cannot myself imagine a sense for it, I cannot even begin to
treat it as a possibility. Do you understand what might be meant by 'moral
consciousness'? Let us say that on a general level of understanding human
moral consciousness is underpinned by the prescription that humans
should not disrespect, much less kill, fellow humans because human
life is precious. But it is abundantly clear that humans have the greatest
difficulty living by it. Indeed, the wise might reproach those who complain
of the failure to comply with the prescription by saying that complainants
should be grateful that the situation is not markedly worse than it is! If
you Androidians were programmed to follow the same prescription, who
is to say that you might not one day question its validity? After all, you are
not yourselves human but are of a different and, you may judge, superior

species of being. If might is right, why should not the superior subdue the inferior and dispense with it altogether?)

Let us return to our question as to whether human life is worthy of preservation in the great scheme of things.

I am reminded of the remarks on this subject made fleetingly but interestingly by a philosopher of my acquaintance. He once raised the question of whether human life should be treated differently from any other form of life on planet Earth concerning the preservation of its existence. Dinosaurs became extinct, as did other species of animal life before them and since. Why should not humankind suffer the same fate?

If humankind is considered merely as species of animal life, the answer to the question is reasonably clear. There is no reason at all to suppose that humankind cannot suffer the same kind fate as any other form of life, plant or animal, with the difference that the fate humans suffer may be said to be at their own hands should they be stupid and wicked enough to engage in a global nuclear war, or stupid and greedy enough to make the planet uninhabitable for themselves.

But if the question involves a *moral dimension* such that it is asking whether human life on planet Earth has about it a *value* that should be preserved, the answer must surely depend on whether or not those to whom the question is directed think it does or not. Those who think it does not have particular value would probably respond with a shrug of the shoulders, while others would be aghast at the very idea that everything humans have achieved should be thrown aside, which is to say that they would have a *sense* of human achievement connected with what they regard as 'civilisation' and a 'civilised' way of life, with achievements in art, music, science, architecture, mathematics, democratic decision making, respect for human life and a myriad of sociological advances. In other words, they would talk of such things in order to establish a moral case for the continuance of human life. Humans, they may say, leave a great deal to be desired, but it does not follow from this that human life is worth nothing at all. We might even say, it is not human life that is being weighed here but what human life is capable of achieving. There is hope here, too. If much good has been achieved already, might there not be more to come?

Now, my dear Androidians, do these sentiments mean anything to you. Do they 'compute'?

The Nineteenth Epistle

Dear Androidians,

I trust you have thought long and well over the formal validity of my reflections so far. But I know I am expecting the impossible due to your inability to comprehend the moral import of those propositions. Any argument which involves the concepts 'progress' and 'improvement' must be incomprehensible to you.

There is perhaps one flaw which I myself have introduced by way of universality and generality, and it must be dealt with. I have suggested that hopes for the moral improvement of humankind are most questionable due to the fact that humans have an animal nature from which they find it impossible to extricate themselves.

Yet here it is easy to fall prey to the universal and the general, for the exceptions may be as important as the rules which they prove. I refer to the ability of some humans to rise above their animal natures even in circumstances where the animal is given every encouragement to predominate and rule over the restraints which normally keep that animal in check. When humans find themselves *in extremis* many nevertheless find within themselves a moral courage to rise above such circumstances even when their very existence is threatened in so doing. Self-sacrifice in war or in poverty, not only for family members but even for strangers, is by no means unknown. Such instances provide examples for others less inclined to follow suit, and in such examples the weaker amongst them may see paradigms of action and self-denial which they can admire and respect even if they find it too difficult to emulate them. Such is the power of individual action, of individual self-sacrifice and self-abnegation.

Indeed, such is the power of the individual that we are tempted to assert that it is through individuals that mass improvement may be made in all walks of human life, in art, in science, in social reforms, in ways of thinking and therefore of acting. It is, we may be tempted to say, individuals who have moved the tide of moral progress onward, individuals who have inspired general trends towards the betterment of human life, not simply pragmatically but in ways of thinking and feeling: writers, reformers, artists, poets, statesmen – it is such as these who have given hope for an improved future.

As against these, we find individuals who in virtue of crooked and perverse thinking have done precisely the opposite by having a retrogressive effect on the society of humans. They have instigated wars and initiated decline.

The battle between the good and the bad can never be terminated. The single hope must always be that the good will prevail over the bad.

If we return now to the universal and the general, we must concede that whether humans will save themselves from destruction, moral or physical or both, must always remain a matter of conjecture. Indeed, whether anyone will exist capable of understanding, explaining and recording the outcome is equally uncertain.

I suppose you Androidians may after all continue to exist, not having the faintest idea about what has happened or why.

But if your heads are buried in the sand, you can hardly be held accountable for that. Humans also strive, most successfully, to mask the realities of the so-called 'human condition'. Even the wise will endeavour to find sufficient distraction in the smallest things, like a tasty morsel or a pleasant drink or a day at the beach, especially so after their dreams have come to nothing or are discovered to be unattainable, or attainable but less attractive than they once seemed. Many humans seek solace in routine, however trivial or even mindless that routine may be. True there is much to be achieved when animal natures are taught to know their place, and herein lies some modicum of hope for some improvements in that condition. But routine furnishes comfort and security of a kind. Having perhaps glimpsed the sunny uplands of improvement, most humans resort again to the familiar and the undemanding flatness of their routines, leaving to more extraordinary and therefore woefully rare individuals the sacrifice and discomfort that profound insight and true virtue requires. As one such individual once said, men sometimes stumble over the truth, but then they almost invariably pick themselves up and continue on their way.

The Twentieth Epistle

My Dear Androidians,

It is inevitable that I must continue to address you on the fragile assumption that you will at least comprehend my reflections on a broad level of generality. Therefore, it will perhaps be clear to you that everything I write is an attempt to understand human life and nature, because much of this life and nature is strange and most distressing to me. I am trying, I confess in vain, to make sense of what humans do and say. I am endeavouring to understand their achievements and their failings and to weigh the one against the other to see which is greater, to see whether the one will outbalance the other, so that I shall be able to say either that there is hope for a better future on planet Earth, or wherever humans will end up residing, or whether such hope is groundless. In all this, then, I am engaged in an attempt to weigh in the balance the moral worth of those creatures with whom I am surrounded and of whom I am myself ostensibly and regrettably one. My conviction that I am not myself one of them would be widely considered unreasoned and unreasonable at best, intolerably presumptuous at worst, a clear example of unforgivable hubris.

Understanding humans is a formidable task, perhaps an impossible one since the variables are innumerable. A loving upbringing is expected to produce a loving human, yet not necessarily so. An unhappy childhood is expected to produce an unhappy human, yet not necessarily so. A cleric who is compassionate towards his parishioners is not necessarily kind to his children. A serial murderer may spare a dog before a human. And are there humans who behave and think as though they were recognisably human only in physical form.

But I must consider more carefully what I mean by 'understanding humans and human behaviour'. What kind of understanding do I lack? What kind of understanding do I seek? What 'understanding' means for me is not I think an understanding of *causes*, for no list of causes, of causes and their effects, or of reasons, can help me to *understand* man's inhumanity to man. When I say that I cannot understand what they do, I mean that I cannot condone what they do, that I can find no moral justification for what they do. The issue with man's inhumanity to man is the impossibility of *accepting* it, of accepting it and then, as they say, of *moving on*. My lack of understanding is akin to the man who says, 'I cannot understand how anyone could possibly ill-treat another.' 'Understanding' means 'moral acceptance'. It is the kind of understanding the lack of which should be applauded. It cannot be *resolved* by any kind of 'science' known to humans, for it is not a question of any science. I must confess, concerning man's inhumanity to man I am in a state of perpetual and irreversible non-acceptance. The idea 'to understand causes is to *explain*' is not the equivalent of 'to understand causes is to *justify*'.

What is to be done to bring about a *universality* of non-acceptance? Can anything be done? And is such a universality even desirable or as desirable as it may appear at first sight? He who asks such questions is like one lost in misty mountains, forever following false trails, backtracking on familiar routes and ending up where he began yet hardly recognising where he first stood and not knowing where his next step should be. The questions themselves are questionable – are they questions, or simply cries of anguish?

But meanwhile, threats of so-called 'limited nuclear intervention' have been made by one state against another, and this has, predictably, been met with the counter-threat of retaliation, although many are contemplating what they call 'a first strike option'. A variety of moral insanity seems to be an inevitable cerebral concomitant of the human creature. Not all become servile to the propensity towards mindless destruction, and these have coined the phrase 'moral blindness' to refer to those who are. But the good and the wise are destroyed by the same weapons that are ranged against the bad and the foolish – the same bullet does for all.

What can be made of all those who talk blandly of nuclear war? Of those who talk and of all those who follow those that talk? And when talking ends and war begins, the endless human capacity for inhumanity is inexplicable.

Is there nothing to be said for humans, in evidence of their virtue? Is there no hope that goodness and wisdom will eventually prevail over wickedness and stupidity? You may think so, Androidians, when you consider the existence of religions amongst humans. Surely their existence is evidence of some virtue, some goodness, a wish to live in peace and mutual respect! But then I must tell you that different religions, despite some common ground, are in perpetual competition and conflict, and, more than this, that some religions seem quite bereft of love; indeed, they seem constrained to find a place in all their texts for the very word, and that in the name of some religions all manner of cruelty is to be found, and that inhumanity flows from religions more readily than respect for human life and dignity. Cruelty, persecution, ignorance and intolerance not only emanate from human religions but are precisely those elements that preserve them and afford them power.

In the constant and unrelenting struggle between good and bad, religion is to be found on both sides and at one and the same time, so that it is hard to see what good religion does for the future of humankind.

If there is hope for the future of humankind, it is to be found in beauty, which is something that religions lack. Ritual and tradition have ousted the beauty that religions might once have boasted, rather like the burgeoning absence of oxygen will eventually snuff out a candle.

My dear Androidians, if there is to be any hope for the future of humankind at large, it is to be found in beauty.

The Twenty-first Epistle

My Dear Androidians,

We must examine the idea of 'beauty'. I must tell you that this subject would merit analyses of considerable length and depth, works such as I truly believe Androidians are still incapable of undertaking. We must proceed by touching upon relatively straightforward examples and hope that they will be comprehensible to the Androidian intellect.

To speak of 'the beauty' of an *idea* is to register approval, acceptance or recommendation. But since, as humans have recognised, beauty is in the eye of the beholder, the value of the thing approved or recommended must be subjective. 'The beauty of it is that…' may expound an enthusiastic recommendation, but one that will be singularly objectionable to those who are unfortunate enough to have to listen to it propounded. Imagine that the proposal is that an entire people should be exterminated. No, the beauty of an idea is a colloquialism that has nothing whatever to do with beauty and is therefore irrelevant to the kind of beauty that might save humanity from its own destruction and others from destruction at the hands of humanity.

Then there is visual beauty, as when humans speak of the beauty of a landscape or of the painting that depicts it. Humans are impressed by colours and shapes and the ways in which light plays upon them and distinguishes them and relates them together. The beauty of the human form is that which stirs the emotions with its sheer physicality and sexuality, for physicality and sexuality go very deep with humans and are capable of transforming, influencing, and even destroying their lives. Such things belong to the animal nature of what it is to be a human being. Humans have little choice but to be impressed, and often vastly over-impressed, by the human form, paying much more attention to it than they do to the health and direction of the human brain and the human mind.

To continue to be impressed by the human physical form and to wonder at the beauty of a landscape and its representation are important, not to say essential, ingredients of a life that is distinctively human. It is important to preserve the *distinctively* human character of human life, for limiting the damage that humans may do to one another must not entail the elimination of that character, for that would be like cutting the head off the patient who complains of toothache in order to relieve him of local discomfort – or like, as they say, throwing the baby out with the bathwater.

Nevertheless, the appreciation of and the attention paid to nature, art and sexuality, will not of themselves prevent humans from destroying one another or others from being destroyed by them. In fact, such attentions are often the stuff of jealous rivalries between individuals and may ultimately result in insufferable tensions and various forms of destruction, mental or physical or both. Jealousy is invariably destructive, and we must find forms of beauty which transcend individual preoccupations with self.

Where shall we find them and what do they look like?

Simplicity is a concept that is not at all simple, yet I shall use the word liberally. You, Androidians, know the word very well. Humans know that the word 'simple' may be applied to a fundamental algebraic axiom like a tautology (a=a), or an elementary equation in arithmetic (2x10

= 4x5). Humans also know that Androidian notions of simplicity are far more complex, so much so that only a very few amongst the human mathematical elite can ever hope to understand Androidian concepts of, say, *algebraic* simplicity. Humans are notoriously lost without their equality sign (=), just as Androidians themselves are puzzled by the cerebral limitations of human mathematicians. Humans have no conception of identity that omits a notion of *equation* expressed by '='.

Thankfully, it is not necessary to examine the concept of simplicity more thoroughly, for the simplicity of the beauty that provides any basis for hope for the future of humankind, and the preservation of Androidian civilisation should that civilisation come into contact with humans, is something that is *felt and shown* rather than a proposition that must be subjected to mathematical scrutiny and the rigours of algebraic logic.

I must suspend any doubts I have concerning your ability to comprehend human concepts. I shall attempt to get you to understand beauty, because it is in beauty that any realistic hope must lie. For humans there is no panacea. For humans there will be no utopia. There is simply the question of damage limitation, the matter of limiting the damage they do to one another and to others. The issue is not so much that of making things better but of things not becoming significantly worse than they are or have ever been. In this, the only hope is the continuing creation and perception of beauty. It is only beauty that can hold the balance between good and evil, between wisdom and stupidity, between knowledge and ignorance.

But it is hard to talk about beauty, for beauty at its best is shown, not described in advance of itself. It is not so much proved as *felt*, and it cannot be felt without first being shown.

Let us start from simple beginnings, for beauty is a house of many mansions as the various uses of the word will testify.

There are humans who will speak of the 'beauty' of mathematics, and they use the word as an expression of approval or attachment. Those who despise mathematics are hardly likely to use the word. Or we might say that the beauty of mathematics consists in the perceived symmetry and logic of, say, the steps towards an algebraic equation or a proof in Euclidean geometry and in the indisputability of the outcome. When the proposition in question is proved and the steps towards it revealed, someone might speak of the beauty of the proof.

Androidians, with the utmost respect to the subject in which you continue to excel and for which you are universally known and admired, the perception of the 'beauty' of mathematics will do nothing to save humanity from itself or save others from the unfortunate excesses of humanity.

Mathematics is merely a tool, and as such can be used for good or for ill. It cannot therefore answer questions about what good is, and, by the same token, cannot define beauty.

The beauty that should concern us is shown in the simple maternal and paternal affections, the natural feelings that parents have towards their offspring, the sacrifices they make for their children and the supreme sacrifices they are prepared to make without hesitation should it ever become necessary to make them.

Lest such an example be considered too 'natural' or 'instinctive' and therefore too close to those inclinations shared by lesser species of animal life, the beauty of which we speak is also shown in simple acts of kindness, such as those shown in the parable of the Good Samaritan, which happens to be the only example of its kind that was programmed into your psyche during your inception. Such simple examples are *felt* by those who witness them, by those who witness them and are *moved* by them, for such acts are capable of moving some humans to tears. But it is not for all to be so moved. That is the rub. The act of holding the hand of a dying human who would otherwise die comfortless is an act of kindness capable of moving those who witness it if, and only if, those who witness it are capable of being so moved. If they are capable of being moved, they are also capable of showing the same kindness to others.

The knowledge, if it is possible to use such a word, of what it is to be kind and to show kindness to others, is shown by example, not by argument, just as the ability to be moved by kindness is possessed as though by *instinct* and not acquired through practice.

The spring of such beauty is of course love. Like beauty, love is a house of many mansions – indeed, it may prove that beauty and love are different names for the same instinct. The love of which we speak is not the instinct for sex although the two are often equated, just as pleasure is often mistaken for happiness.

If the perception, and therefore creation, of beauty is an instinct enlivened by example and not inculcated by theoretical instruction, it would seem to follow that it is to be found universally in all humans. Yet it is clear that not all humans are equally capable of the perception of beauty or the capacity to love, for there are many who enjoy war as though it were a sport, cruelty as though it were a harmless pastime, torture as though it were a form of salutary therapy. Clearly, the perception of beauty as we have loosely defined it is not to be identified with the perception of beauty in a piece of music or in art, for history shows us that the most bestial of humans are capable of artistic appreciation and the love of music. This granted, is it any wonder that moral progress amongst humans has been described as one step forward and two steps back?

Human capacities are not equally shared. This fact is one of the hardest to grasp, and it is one that you Androidians must endeavour with every ounce of your cerebral powers to come to terms with. A hard task indeed, and one which, as I have often explicitly stated, you may not be capable of undertaking let alone completing.

This analysis, threadbare and incomplete as it must inevitably be, brings me to what may be considered a dichotomy between *doing* and *waiting*. I believe this dichotomy to be a *false* one.

Since the capacity to perceive and therefore create beauty is not universally possessed, and certainly not universally possessed to the same degree, there is much to be said for the notion that the moral progress of humankind is something that cannot be forced or coerced but needs to come almost of its own accord – just as a wilful child is expected to improve with time, since no amount of coercion or no number of blandishments can bring about moral improvement. Such a view has about it at least a *prima facie* validity. Does this mean then that nothing can be *done*?

No. What is done is to teach by example. The child absorbs beauty by osmosis through example. At least, this is a reasonable expectation, since what is probably called a 'growing maturity' transforms wilfulness into moral responsibility and a respect for others. I say 'reasonable expectation'. I do not say 'absolute certainty'. Therefore, *waiting* does not exclude *doing*.

Force and coercion cannot by themselves bring about a lasting and significant moral advance, let alone a utopia. The history of human revolutions amply testify as much. It has been truly said that a revolution is one man holding a gun to another man's head – an observation delightfully pithy but regrettably valid.

More than this, when *waiting and doing* is applied to the whole human race, I fear that no amount of waiting and no amount of doing will change the human race *en bloc* for the better, which is why ventured earlier that amongst humans there will never be a utopia, never a final and lasting resolution of the fight between good and bad, between light and dark. On the canvas of human destiny we can expect nothing better than shades of murky grey. One poet once said of his people that they are delightful in the particular but obnoxious in the generality. Much the same can be said of the human race as a whole.

Therefore Androidians, the very best you are entitled to expect from humans is that you have the very good and very rare fortune to be approached by humans who tend to walk more in the light than in darkness. There are indeed such as these. If you meet them, hold fast to them, as they must hold fast to their precepts lest they be overtaken by the dark forces that are perpetually at work against them.

Humans there are who do hold to high precepts, and it is precisely these, though in the minority, who hold the balance against opposing forces. Each human, you must understand, stands alone, but no human stands alone as much as those who strive to hold to the highest precepts, for such precepts are constantly under threat, not only from external forces, but even from their holders, since the temptation to betray what they most cherish is forever lurking in the background of their own psyches. Loneliness is hardest to endure when the light struggles hardest against the shadows and the advocates of much lesser precepts hold out a hand of friendship albeit false and so easily corruptible.

There is another sense in which each human must stand alone, and his standing alone can be the spring of both good and evil. This I shall attempt to explain in my next communication. Meanwhile, Androidians, I wish you tranquillity and productive meditation.

The Twenty-second Epistle

Dear Androidians,

In my last communication I claimed that each human is necessarily alone and that his perception of his being so can be the spring of either good or evil.

Perceiving that they are alone in experiencing their own pain and, ultimately, in experiencing their own demise, humans may decide to pursue selfish aims whenever and wherever they can escape punishment or censure in doing so. They see no point and little comfort in the notion of 'the common good' and find more than sufficient reason to pursue their own individual good without limit.

Then there are humans who, equally recognising their own mortality, believe it necessary in virtue of this to pursue selfless aims, and they see more than sufficient reason to attach the greatest priority to love, togetherness and the common good, for they believe this to be the best way to live with the fact that they must die. The pain of grief and loss is a reason to band together in mutual affection, instead of pursuing individual ambitions irrespective of whether they harm or benefit others. It is tempting to say that the root of mutual kindness is a recognition, conscious or otherwise, of the futility of conflict in a context in which each human must share the same fate and in which the blind pursuit of self-interest must itself first appear base and baseless and then irrelevant. An obsession with the amassing of riches will at least become questionable if the riches amassed cannot be transferred to an afterlife or cannot even be properly and uncritically enjoyed in the life that at present exists.

Here we must take account of religions that promise an afterlife to those who live selflessly. Such a promise seems to straddle the two categories mentioned above, in that the tendency to pursue selfish aims in view of the finality of ceasing to exist is mitigated by the promise of an extension of life after death. The fact that humans are in grave error by taking such promises seriously and literally is irrelevant. What is relevant is simply their *perception* that these promises are to be taken seriously and literally. The very existence of the notion of an afterlife is a restraint on the tendency otherwise to pursue entirely selfish aims at the expense of the common or individual good. Any religion that promises an afterlife is in fact attempting to impose a restraining order on irresponsible and exclusively self-centred behaviour, not of course that the hierarchies of such religions would see and put the matter in such terms, for they are themselves deeply and irretrievably mesmerised by the illogicality of the promises they happily and unreservedly expound and promulgate.

The fear of extinction can therefore be the spring of either selfish or selfless behaviour, and in the same human is habitually the source of both, since no human can boast perfection in either and every human is subject to the oscillations of temper and mood to which the human condition subjects him.

Androidians would do well to remember that the inescapability of death, and its finality, especially to those who hold no belief in an afterlife, is indeed a fact too heavy for humans to bear with perfect equanimity. It is the cause of much distress and anxiety and often contaminates the plans, aspirations and hopes of all who must take it into sober consideration, not to mention the depths of abject grief and loneliness of spirit into which humans must inevitably be plunged many times in their relatively short lives. This is at least one aspect of the human condition that Androidians can never hope to comprehend. Be assured however that humans, the very good or the very bad, and *all* humans, who are *both* good in part and bad in part, would deserve your deepest sympathies were you fully capable of affording them.

The Twenty-third Epistle

Dear Androidians,

I continue to hope that my communications are beginning to bear some fruit and that you are able to form some idea of the concept of beauty, for I have said that without beauty, its perception and creation, the warnings I began to issue you concerning human intrusion are too likely to prove valid, and that with the slow demise of beauty the future of humankind itself will be in grave doubt.

Granted the enormous importance of this concept, I think it might be worthwhile to examine what I believe to be a species of beauty, namely friendship.

True friendship is the primacy of want over need, to be wanted irrespective of being needed. The zombification of the human psyche has rendered the perception of such distinctions more difficult than ever before. Technical dexterity has been confused with intellectual competence, just as pleasure has been confused with happiness, and mere acquaintance with friendship. Push-button agility and so-called 'screen fluency' has replaced the capacity for independent, and therefore critical, thought. In this way, humans have allowed themselves to become zombified, and the process of zombification is by now almost complete, giving rise to a downward spiral of moral and cerebral metamorphosis.

True friendship is a species of beauty insofar as it is an expression of love, and with the word 'love' no idle sentimentality is intended. Friendship is one human putting another before himself; it means a readiness for self-sacrifice, and the capacity to feel pleasure in the success of this other in the realisation of his hopes, dreams or ambitions provided they are deemed righteous, and a readiness to dispute or even condemn them if they are not.

Friendship is a species of that kind of beauty that is capable of saving humankind if, and only if, it is universally, or at least sufficiently widely, shared.

But here is the rub. The rigour of Androidian logic is hardly required to conclude that hope grounded in true friendship is at best precarious, at worst impossible. Instead, the balance between hope and despair, like that between good and evil, must be maintained sufficiently to avoid a steep descent into an oblivion total and irreversible.

All of which is simply another way of announcing that human life is what it is. Conflict is in the very nature of opposing forces, and opposition is integral to human life, past, present and future. No panacea and no utopia on any visible horizon can be discerned, because none is ever even discernible by eyes human or otherwise.

The consolation is that such a conclusion, if granted, does not deny that true friendship exists. It simply states that it is not strong enough, not universal enough to ensure the safe and untroubled future of humankind. Humankind is forever fated to walk a tightrope, and the balance maintained along it can with every further step be lost.

It is not as though true friendship between humans and between nations has been lost, for it never was in the ascendant let alone in abundance. It was ever an ideal to be pursued as an ideal and seldom if ever considered a reality just waiting to materialise with only a little extra effort. An extraordinary human to whom even sainthood was granted, St Augustine of Hippo, once remarked that a true friend was one to whom the secrets of the heart might be vouchsafed – but such a friend is rare indeed, and more a template from the shadowy world of Platonic forms than a reality to be met with albeit rarely.

Nevertheless, my dear Androidians, we may assert with sufficient authority that the species of beauty which the ideal of true friendship exemplifies is that which is capable of saving humankind from humankind, or non-humankind from humankind. We may therefore reiterate our warnings to you and be glad that you may, even through a glass darkly, see reason to be on your best guard against the hypocrisies of mankind. The beauty that is, would be or might be, capable of ensuring a lastingly better world for humans and those for whom they may come into contact is in lamentably short supply, an irreversible deficiency aided and abetted if not directly caused by zombification of the human psyche – a process that is too serious to be the object of humorous derision.

The Twenty-fourth Epistle

Dear Androidians,

The statement I made at the end of my last letter was not at all intended to suggest that you yourselves might consider the demise of the human intellect in consequence of zombification a matter for merriment or light-hearted comment. Of course not – if only because you are quite incapable of humour. You were at no point endowed with a sense of humour, a faculty useless to you, but quite indispensable to humans.

Humour is as multifaceted as human nature itself. It can be the balm of the very human condition of which it is the effect, arising as it does from the perception that death and extinction without exception and reprieve is the one feature of the human condition that enjoys mathematical certainty. To make light of the inevitable is sometimes an emotional release. It can also be a poisonous barb, a weapon to unleash at the deserving and the undeserving alike. It may be a way of allowing humans to laugh at themselves – an extremely healthy pastime, though not one of which all humans are capable, since many take themselves so seriously that to smile at themselves would seem to threaten their very identity or create fissures in their elevated perceptions of self. One human's object of humour is another's expression of profound and unforgivable felony, especially in matters of politics and religion, given that the latter in particular is also a balm to so many of its adherents and therefore enjoys a sanctity that removes it from the library of comedy and installs it on a pinnacle so high that the eagles themselves become breathless in any attempt to circumnavigate it and fall like stones to more common ground where they lie gasping but grateful for their swift descent.

One human's joke is another human's cause for bitter resentment. But the wry humour of the wise when perceiving the conceits of their fellows, their selfish ambitions and their pursuit of wealth and fame, is not understood by all, or at least not accepted by them as a guide to righteous living. On the contrary, and as I have observed already, there are many who observing the fleeting nature of life would take this as a licence to do as they please provided they do not break what they humorously call the Eleventh Commandment, namely that they should avoid discovery and therefore evade punishment or the blandishments of their betters.

Since the zombification of the human psyche humour has not escaped a steady demise. That an event or fact is funny is no longer cause to find it so – and this alone is enough to turn humour on its head, to banish it to some unknown realm, to abolish it as though it were an ugly institution, useless and long past its sell-by date. Humour was once a useful tool to cut down to size the horrific pretensions of a dictator or tyrant, to put such as these in their place and discredit and belittle their vile ambitions, and because of this such species of humour was outlawed in dictatorships and tyrannies. But the job has been so well and universally done that now there is nothing left to outlaw. Zombification has completed the task that formerly fell to dictators and tyrants. It all began with the 'doctoring' of language, ostensibly in order to avoid causing offence to the sensibilities of humans who allegedly possessed them. In this, as in many other areas of human endeavour, the road to hell is paved with confused intentions.

Zombies are incapable of laughing at themselves, nor do they find objectionable the excesses of political and religious doctrine. Zombies find themselves all at sea, scowls and sneers of discontent have replaced smiles and good-natured peels of laughter, for humour has lost all intelligence and wisdom and is now the nothing but the outpourings of the ignorant and the dispossessed.

Well, my dear Androidians, you are totally incapable of adjudicating these judgements, of measuring their validity, of disputing their truth, of revealing their flaws and their falsities. You are not competent to judge whether 'Humans are masters of their own fate' is or is not the best joke ever uttered.

I cannot decide whether such an incapacity is to your advantage or not. Neither can you. Suffice to say that a sense of humour amongst humans may be graded from the most base to the most incisive, from the simple to the complex, from the most unhelpful to the most beneficial. But the best that a sense of humour can offer is as subject to the degenerative misfortunes of human life as anything else – a decline in intelligence, in wisdom, in compassion, in respect for others, will reveal itself in what humans find humorous, in what they laugh at. Such decline may even determine whether they laugh at all – whether they even retain the capacity to laugh. But let us also remember that no-one has ever heard laughter amongst the Androidians, and that any laughter heard would cause the utmost consternation amongst humans. Have you ever thought of this, my dear Androidians? After all, you were all zombified from the very outset and were, and have subsequently proved, incapable of thinking anything about it. A sense of humour has never been an item in your consideration. Yet I see you have managed to live peacefully without it. Or am I mistaken? Humour is outlawed when humans grieve over the loss of their loved ones, for grief fills the human psyche leaving no room for anything else. Humour and unquenchable sorrow, like oil and water, do not mix. Do you suppose then that when humans grieve they become like Androidians in their immunity to humour? Yet they are *not* Androidians and are therefore to be unreservedly pitied for the tortuous pains they must bear, for they are not immune to the blinding, paralysing pain of loss – zombification has not progressed so far as to extricate humans from profound grief when those close to them and define them cease to exist and become like shadows in a dream.

The Twenty-fifth Epistle

Dear Androidians,

We have by now perhaps explained how humans are subject to two forces: they are assailed by nature, by the warming of the planet which they themselves, at least in part, have unwittingly caused, for this no doubt is nature's revenge for years of mindless abuse; and they are assailed directly by themselves through war and a continuum of inhumanities.

Yet, what use is there to catalogue human errors, deficiencies and failings, if we are not to ask what there is to be done, or wonder whether there is *anything* to be done?

Yet perhaps there is at least something that might be done to good effect. It has been said by the wise that the acknowledgement of error is the beginning of wisdom. The error is grounded in this, that humans are clever enough to invent and devise new technologies, in particular artificial intelligence, but not astute enough to remain its master. Clever enough, but demonstrably not *good* enough. The ability to remain master of what is created requires above all moral intelligence. But moral intelligence has been sapped by the extraordinary zeal for so-called 'progress'. The moral compass has been lost with the inability to clarify ends, the consequent lack of morally critical appraisal of objectives, and the malaise attendant upon the contempt for self-criticism.

But a precondition of the acknowledgement of error is the possession of Soul. I introduce the word with a capital letter, wishing thereby to indicate that it is meant to represent a distillation, as it were, of moral values, or, better, that it is intended to be an umbrella term for such values that are opposed to or which at least mitigate, greed, selfishness, obsession with self-interest and the attachment of primacy to sexual attraction and physical intercourse. We must be content with a rough approximation when defining Soul since the concept is not intended to be used in any theological or metaphysical sense. Its usefulness lies in its generality, for it is not a name for any specific object.

What is said of 'soul' may also be said of 'spirituality', for the spirituality of humans does not necessarily connote any religious affiliation or bent but is meant to suggest a moral capacity as distinct from the purely instinctive. It may also be said in passing that those who stress the animal in humans are likely to underestimate the spiritual, while those who stress the spiritual are equally likely to underestimate the animal.

It has been observed by the more thoughtful amongst humans that the distinguishing feature of humans is the possession of soul and that this differentiated them from Androids, for Androids could never be said to possess soul. But since talk of the duality of soul and body was unwelcome with the slow but steady demise of religion and its mythologies and metaphysics amongst, in particular, the 'science' fraternity, the word 'soul' fell out of favour and was treated with contempt, finally being forgotten in the dark and dusty 'nursery of human development' to which all notions primitive, archaic and simply, though perhaps not demonstrably, nonsensical were ultimately relegated. Humans were left with the singularity of body, bereft of soul.

With the demise of soul came the loss of beauty and its creation anew. The only beauty now extant is that to be found in the past, but humans are never encouraged to look back, only forward, unfortunately into an abyss that looms ahead and for which they are totally unprepared. The future is therefore bereft of promise, a veritable desert of lost opportunities and mindless error.

All of which paints a doomsday scenario. For in the absence of soul, what remains are the animal instincts for survival and procreation. While in the human gut may be found the root causes of disease, so too in the human animal will be found the roots of conflict and inhumanity.

If humans have become deficient in soul, what then is the difference between humans and Androidians? Have humans become the very Androidians they made to serve them and then exiled to Androidia?

If there is no way back, if soul cannot be restored to the human psyche, then humanity is already lost and there is little point in further remonstrance and there is really nothing more to say. My warnings to you, dear Androidians, comes to no more than this: that should erstwhile humans torment you, you will at least be tormented by your own kind! Yet, not so, for the so-called 'instincts' for survival and procreation are what clearly distinguish humans from Androids. Androids are not bedevilled by such instincts, and now, with the steady demise of soul, humans and Androids are more sharply and clearly distinguishable one from the other than ever before. The disadvantage for Androidians, however, is equally clear. Since they are not driven either by the desire for self-survival or procreation, their ability to defend themselves from creatures that are so driven is weakened to zero. Hence my attempts to warn you against the worst of human endeavours is both necessary and futile – necessary because you are incapable of defending yourselves, futile because you have no conception that you should be defended and have no desire to be so.

And hence it is in the nature of such attempts that they resemble the task of squaring the circle.

But should this doomsday scenario be reconsidered? Can the worst on offer be reversed? Can there yet be grounds for hope, can a case still be made for hopefulness in a world bereft of soul? If the soul in humans can be restored, at least in part, there may still be grounds for hope – hope for the survival of humanity and for Androidians, even if the latter cannot even conceptualise the need for it.

First we must ask: how is the loss of soul to be understood, and how is it to be measured? Greed, selfishness and the obstinate obsession with self-interest – is it in these that the loss of soul consists? If so, can the soul in humans be restored even when the animal in their corporeal frame is not merely in the ascendant but reigns supreme?

Is it a panacea we seek? If so, there is nothing to find, only a chimera to aim at, a straw to grasp, a mere shadow to embrace. What then can be done? Can *anything* be done?

It is important to understand that the slow demise of soul was a consequence of the unquestioned idolatry of the machine in the form of artificial intelligence. Humans failed to realise that their burgeoning stupidity was consequent upon their increasing reliance on digital systems, and that therefore the true object of their fears was they themselves. Put simply: humans forget how to think critically and therefore how to reason, how to judge and therefore how to prioritise. They became incapable of putting artificial intelligence in its place. Artificial intelligence took over the function of thinking simply because humans allowed it to do so. It was not so much that AI became vastly intelligent on its own accord and in its own right as that humans themselves declined in intelligence. It was natural therefore that artificial intelligence would produce fake news, fake people, fake governments consisting of fake departments and fake departmental ministers, fake incitement to hatred – a fake world with consequences for the real world which were disastrous. The real world and the fake world were once in fierce competition, until they finally merged into one amorphous and incurable tumour. The stage was set in which independent and objective thinking became almost unachievable – almost, but so hard to achieve that only the most able and the most committed could engage in the herculean task. The potential for unthinking acceptance was always extant, but technological innovation in the form of advanced artificial intelligence caused it to accelerate like an aggressive cancer amongst a world population that was deficient in immunity and all too ready to be consumed by outdated and ruinous forms of ignorance, bigotry and backwardness.

The restoration of soul, insofar as this is now at all possible, requires the faculty of critical judgement to be restored, and this in turn requires as a precondition the restoration of human intelligence.

It is human intelligence and the consequent critical faculty that must lay the groundwork for the restoration of moral judgement and therefore of soul. For the restoration of soul will not be achieved by the invention of an alternative religion. Yet another religion will only sow the seeds of conflict and contempt. No new religion can improve on the ethics of religions already extant, given that it is possible to derive a moral common denominator from them and given that the bad ethics they expound can be easily identified and expunged. There would be no unanimity concerning what are good or bad elements in any new religion, either.

To advocate a new religion is nonsense since it could only ever succeed in further disunity and mindless, ignorant contest. It is clear that the soul has been neglected, if not ejected, from some religions already extant, for they are now tragically deficient in the love they might once have professed and have become clubs whose members merely mouth words by rote as those words alone can save them from the torments of a fiery underworld which they believe is the lot of what they call 'non-believers' or 'infidels'. Inconsequential routine and stagnant ritual has replaced any soul that might otherwise have taken root. A new religion would simply fan the flames of the undying fires of hell.

Talk of a new religion may be compared with that of political revolution, for both religions and revolutions spark only controversy, dissent and discontent. History shows that a revolution that actually takes place is doomed to fail, for even its moral leadership is far from infallible while the masses they lead lack the spirit which the revolution demands for its success. It seems to be an inexorable law that disillusionment is the ungrateful child of vast social change.

If it is thought that only a religion bereft of theology and metaphysics and full of high principles is the only religion worth considering, it should be remembered that humans have had high principles in abundance. The difficulty has never been a scarcity of moral principles, but that they have never put into practice the principles they already professed to have.

Due to the loss of soul engendered by artificial intelligence this 'professorial' fraternity has declined to zero. This fraternity, which has never been able to boast a large membership, has been accompanied by the development of a general neurosis amply exemplified in the tendency to apologise for historical events for which the apologists could not possibly have had any moral responsibility whatsoever, and so apology is confused with regret. The pluralisation of gender, both confused and confusing, is also a consequence of a neurosis masquerading under the banner of sensitivity and awareness. These developments are unmistakable characteristics, indelible markers, of the loss of judgement consequent upon a decline in intelligence or a further decline in intelligence amongst humans who were not endowed with much intelligence to begin with. The markers, though indelible, are invisible to the eyes of those who suffer the neuroses of so-called 'sensitivity' and 'historical responsibility', for these neuroses are themselves a species of moral blindness.

And now, dear Androidians, we must ask again, what is to be done? I rather doubt that we are any closer to answering the question how the soul in humans can be restored and how thereby the animal in man can to a better degree be domesticated without of course eliminating it entirely for then we should merely have disembodied spirits and nothing at all that we could properly call 'human'. How can humanity be saved while remaining entirely *human*?

We must strive to follow in the next epistle whatever of the *logos* remains, though I continue to doubt how much of it falls within your cerebral jurisdiction.

The Twenty-sixth Epistle

Dear Androidians,

I trust that you are all well and that you have not yet surrendered to the temptation to consider my communications either starkly irrelevant to your future stability or, even worse, entirely nonsensical.

I think it helpful to restate briefly the main assertions made so far:

For humans, the faculty of intelligent judgement is a precondition of wisdom, but the decline in the quality of this faculty has tended to make humans progressively more vulnerable to the less desirable elements of humanity. Wars, nuclear war being without doubt the most mindless of all, are therefore not significantly less likely with the passage of time. On the contrary, the prospect of nuclear war seems nearer than it has ever been. The force of argument continues to prove subservient to the argument of force. Humans have become extremely vulnerable to the moral weaknesses of the worst amongst them. The human race has become a danger to itself. By biological analogy, it is as though the immune system has begun to attack itself. Humanity is threatened by its own Trojan Horse of artificial intelligence – a destructive creative of its own making which has reduced the human capacity for independent and critical thought. Independent and critical thinking has never in all places and at all times been the goal of recognisable systems of education. Tyrants and dictators have sought to expunge it from the court of human endeavour – not a very difficult task when the instrument of fear is so readily and universally available and so easily applied. And even in the absence of tyranny and dictatorship independence of mind was not only intellectually difficult to pursue and achieve but was also attended by scorn and calumny and rewarded with ignorant and bigoted reproach and dissension.

And now here, Androidians, I believe we should introduce the notion of a moral *continuum* at one pole of which there is the best that humanity can be, and at the other the worst that humanity can be. At the centre of such a continuum we might imagine the balance between good and bad, the kind of equilibrium to which I have alluded several times already. If the position on the continuum is in favour of the best that humanity can be, that is *above* equilibrium, peace and progress may not only be maintained but expected to move forward progressively. If there is only equilibrium, then matters may go either way. If things stand at a point *below* equilibrium, the future of humanity may be in grave doubt.

There are those amongst the better and indeed best of humanity who have put their faith in *education*. They speak of the importance of a 'good' or a 'proper' education, and what they mean is that the touchstone of such an education is that out of it should come the unassailable conviction that the very concept of war between humans must, without question, be relegated to the primitive, infantile annals of human history. They would say that, for want of a better phrase, 'beauty of soul' should have primacy over the acquisition of skills or the knowledge of mere facts, though they would not deny the importance of skills and the cerebral accumulation of data.

The advocates of such an education would say that the place on the moral continuum at least *at* but hopefully *above* the point of equilibrium would be most served by an education that places absolute priority on the moral decency and wisdom of its graduates. One writer went so far as to say that pupils and students who are not *morally bettered* by their studies have wasted their time and would better find employment in menial labour and live like hermits where they can do as little injury to their fellows as possible, and this despite their possibly having achieved academic distinction!

Well, my dear Androidians, you will not perhaps be surprised to hear that this fellow was pilloried in the court of public opinion and downtrodden in the groves of academe for what were considered to be nothing more than inane yet possibly harmful eccentricities.

Debates may be tiresome but they should continue, and it is well that they should, even if they are without conclusion. The very fact that such matters as the purpose of education should be the subject of reasoned thought and the cerebral cut and thrust is a testimony not only to their intrinsic importance but to the awareness of that importance by those who enter into such debates. When awareness of their importance is no longer evident, the moral balance, places at or above the point of moral equilibrium, are in danger of being forfeited and perhaps lost forever – or, rather, the absence of serious and enduring debate is an indicator that moral equilibrium has already been lost. If debate is not possible, perhaps because it is not permitted, then either there is universal and unanimous agreement on one side or the other, hopefully on the right side, or else the moral compass has lost its polarity.

That said, I shall not enter into the debate here. The proposition that a good person is preferable to one who is merely skilled or merely knowledgeable has much to commend it. But I should think that being a good person and being a skilled or knowledgeable person are not mutually exclusive. If they are not mutually exclusive then a 'good' or 'proper' education should aim to produce people who are both.

However, to aim at something is not necessarily to succeed in achieving it. The variables are many and they are complex. A sense of decency, of responsibility, of compassion, of integrity are qualities which carry no guarantee either of coming into being or of permanence, which is not to say of course that no attempt should be made to instil them.

The course of human history to date shows a constant ebb and flow between below and above the point of equilibrium on the moral continuum postulated. Sometimes and in some places wicked forces are in the ascendant, sometimes and in some places they are in retreat though never entirely extinguished, as indeed forces for good are sometimes and in some places in the ascendant and sometimes and in some places are in retreat though never entirely extinguished.

It is always been a question of *degree*, of variation and of gradation, and usually the variations and gradations have been imperceptible or almost so, rather like the slow and occasional movements and effusions of a volcano long before eruption, and no victory on either side is either absolute or lasting, while time and again a kind of reluctant compromise is the best that can be expected. A war may be devastating, but although those who are wicked are vanquished by those who are good, the buildings left standing may still smoulder out of sight and the dead are a continuing source of grief and of desire for revenge or reprisal. The seeds of the next war are invariably planted in the battlegrounds of the last. It has been well-documented, though not so well believed, that wars solve nothing.

You must be reminded, Androidians, that humans are the worst possible students, for lessons are so easily forgotten, so easily unlearned.

Humans stand once again on the crossroads where the wrong turning may prove fatal. Once again, the wise amongst them rail against the very idea of war and the rest turn towards them a deaf ear. If the point of equilibrium is lost and humans slide to the wrong end of the continuum, those who are wise and those who have simply escaped destruction will be looking to planet Androidia with unprecedented relish, a relish fuelled by the most primitive instinct of all – survival.

Once again we must ask, are there any grounds for hope that equilibrium, at least, can be protected and that movement on the moral continuum may even be reversed in the right direction, thus safeguarding planet Earth and at least lessening the risk that too much attention is paid to Androidia?

Is it sufficient to hope that the best amongst humans may at least outweigh the worst? Complete destruction of the planet has not yet occurred. Global nuclear war has not yet been entered upon. Is it sufficient to hope that common sense will prevail? The grounds are pragmatic. The intense use of nuclear weapons will destabilise the planet for the victors as much as for the losers. It is a war in which there are no victors. Is this outcome sufficient grounds for hope that a universal pragmatism will prevail?

Appeals to 'beauty of soul' and talk of a 'good' or 'proper' education will hardly avail, since the meaning of such words are themselves subject to interpretation. Humans must ultimately be moved by *pragmatism*.

I would ask whether you are disappointed with the assertion that humans are ultimately moved by nothing other than pragmatism, and whether you expected something altruistic, or even religious, such as the now increasingly rarely cited 'sanctity' of human life. But I am reminded that Androidians cannot be disappointed, for there can be no disappointment without expectation, and Androidians are not equipped to cope with expectation other than the expectations to be had in applied mathematics. In any case, we should do well to remember that survival is the ultimate precondition of the sanctity of human life, or of any life at all whether or not it is said to have sanctity. After all, on a planet devoid of all life there can be no sanctitude any more than sanctuary.

(As a suggestive side note, the phrase 'sanctity of human life' has slipped out of currency amongst present-day politicians, no doubt as a consequence of the demise of the importance attached to major religions in the halls of political power. No self-respecting tyrant or dictator would want to be caught out espousing the divine nature of human existence lest he be taken too seriously and the masses begin asking for the source and righteousness of tyrannical authority – such issues were fought over centuries ago and are not likely to be repeated in a future that now appears increasingly bleak and in a present that is increasingly authoritarian, for authority is now unquestionably human, and God and gods are very much out of favour. Naturally, in former times, if tyrants, dictators and war-mongers ever did make reference to the 'sanctity of human life', the phrase was simply one of many in their vast lexicon of hypocrisy and deceit.)

And so, when the terrible prospect of global nuclear war is contemplated, neither a recognition of the beauty of the human soul nor the sanctity of human life will save humans from pulling the nuclear lever. For the lever is not in the hands of saints or clerics. Instead, pragmatism is the argument that most appeals to those who hold the levers of destruction.

But if there is life, we must ask what it is that makes life worth living at all? And here, the beauty of the soul re-enters the stage. Why? How? We must now address ourselves to these questions, dear Androidians.

The Twenty-seventh Epistle

Dear Androidians,

We must continue our quest for hope on a planet in which the roots of hope seem to have perished and the seeds of renewed hope are reluctant to germinate. If there is hope for humans, there is hope for Androidians too, and, if we can find grounds for it, my warnings to you may simply remain hypothetical and have far less the character of firm predictions.

I have walked the streets of cities, and I have seen in the faces of humans the potential for grief, the kind of grief I have many times referred to in my communications with you, and perhaps in the potential for grief there is also the potential for hope.

It is true that the animal nature of humans is often in the ascendant, and also true that no human can remain human unless his animal nature is assumed. But this does not make a human an animal. Animals are not endowed with compassion, and compassion grows out of the capacity for grief, and grief is deepest where there is love. For as long as humans retain the capacity to grieve, there will be hope that wars will cease. When love dies, all hope dies with it. Grief a human feels for the loss of another is a sure indicator of love.

When love dies, grief dies, and when grief dies, compassion dies. The continuing capacity to feel the pain of loss implies the continuance of hope, for the pain of loss implies the existence of love. Inhumanity is an attempt to deny that love carries the highest possible price, rather like someone who attempts to cheat the shopkeeper by replacing the right price tag with one that is cheaper – successive attempts may be made but they will always ultimately fail for as long as the price of love remains at a premium.

There are always humans for whom talk of love and compassion will always be little more than an over indulgence in fanciful notions. Yet such realities provide the only grounds for hope for the continued and by and large amicable existence of humans on planet Earth, other than appeals to stark pragmatism. Love and pragmatism may be a winning combination; neither one negates the other, for they are not mutually exclusive, but nor are they synonymous, for only love allows of self-sacrifice, while pragmatism is the protection and survival of selfhood. Yet few subjects can claim to be as important as the survival of humankind, for without humankind what is there to talk about? Not love, not compassion, not pragmatism, either. There is no assurance whatsoever that any living creatures, other than human, found in this universe or any other have developed such concepts as love and compassion. My attempt to convey such notions to you Androidians is troubled with doubts. That is why my own reflections move now forward, now backward, for I am like one who walks gingerly, without compass or direction, in a dark and unexplored forest fraught with dangers.

Some humans have said that all of their kind are 'just passing through' what they consider to be 'this vale of tears'. But, if true, it would be easier to pass through *together*, not *against* each other.

How can a sense of universal fraternity, of comradeship, be fostered and sustained?

Perhaps, dear Androidians, the problem is this, that we are looking for certainty where there can be no certainty. Humans invented mathematics, but the future of humanity is not a mathematical certainty. Humans themselves may be counted, but they are not mathematical entities. The best that we can achieve in our reflections on the future of humanity is probability. But it is precisely the probability of future events that troubles us and that therefore should trouble you.

If probability must replace certainty, so too must the particular replace generalisation. Generalisation is simple, and what is simple is easy, and this is presumably why the tendency to generalise is hard to resist. What may be true of many humans is not necessarily true of all. Many humans are afraid of ending up alone, but for many humans living alone may be more desirable than sharing a life with others. It is wrong to speak of what all humans think or want just as it is wrong to speak of what all humans do. What is tolerable for some is intolerable for others. What some call good others call bad. Yet between opposites there has been something approaching an equilibrium, at least until now. In other words, the forces for good have generally and largely succeeded in holding the fort against the forces for bad. But to speak of what all humans are capable or incapable of, to speak of the future of the human race as if it were a prognosis equally applicable to each and every human, is surely mistaken. It is all very well for well-meaning clerics and academic philosophers to fantasise about the brotherhood of man, but that brotherhood does not extend to all humans and, at present, the membership of the brethren is in serious and perhaps irreversible decline. The values that define that fraternity, principally the 'sanctity' of life, respect for others, compassion and egalitarianism, are not universally shared or even understood let alone practised, and even those who espouse such values more often than not fail to live by them.

Hope concerning the future of anything worthy of the name 'morally robust civilisation' must really acknowledge the threadbare patchwork of humankind. The best that can be hoped for is that the balance of good and evil is at least maintained and that it does not incline too much under the weight of the latter. If good is in the ascendant it cannot be expected to remain so for long, let alone in a state of permanence. The threadbare patchwork that is humankind is mirrored in moral geography, with some nations backward and under cruel, inhumane governance, and other nations which, though more humane and less cruel, are nevertheless far from perfect models of moral enlightenment. Perfection is not something that belongs to human life, even if perfection were an intelligible concept, which I am sure it is not. A life of moral perfection may be the lot of some rare individuals, but it is not something that has anywhere near general application. Moral perfection, if difficult to find in an individual life, is infinitely harder to imagine in a state composed of millions. And all this even if 'moral perfection' made sense, which I know it does not.

All this talk of moral perfection is unintelligible to you Androidians, and your excuse is that you have no concept of moral imperfection. But it is also unintelligible to me. The plain truth of the matter is that hope for the future of humankind can be no more than a wish that it proceeds just as it does now, that it becomes no worse than it is now, that deterioration will never be sufficient to bring about the end of humanity in favour of the purely animal, and that the purely animal will not press the buttons and pull the levers of total annihilation. Such is the sad realism that an assessment of the grounds for hope must entail.

And so Androidians, it is becoming sufficiently plain that my warnings to you continue to have validity. My hopes on your behalf consist in this, that humans will not give in to their baser natures and seek to overwhelm you, exploit you and wish you gone with more than adequate means to see it done.

The human template for such behaviour is easily seen in history, in events that have been amply recorded, though who can tell how old, how ancient, the template is, for there is much wickedness that has been done that remains unrecorded and forevermore unknown. One or two examples will suffice here, but I promise you they make for grim reading. From them some humans have spoken of lessons learned. But I am afraid humans make recalcitrant students when it comes to learning from past inhumanities. Yet it seems that these 'errors', if we choose to call them such, were inevitable given that there was and is no cure for human nature that is universally known, and even where known rarely practised, by humankind. Goodness, we must remember, is in the gift of individuals, not in the possession of nations or of humans in the generality.

Attempts to forcefully remove, relocate, decimate or even exterminate whole peoples such as the Jews, Native North Americans and the Armenians, not to mention many much lesser-known instances of heinous inhumanity, all left their indelible marks not only on the pages of history books but on the consciences of nations. Thankfully, all such attempts failed to achieve their full potential, although the Native Americans, for the most part, survived by ceasing, through 'assimilation' to be Native Americans. They failed because, as most humans prefer to believe, contrary forces proved successful in the defence of human values. But there is always a next time, and next time the outcome could be disastrous for humankind in general. Optimism is at best seasoned with a little salt, with a sober appreciation of the known facts of recorded history. Sanity amongst humans is, like common sense, sparsely distributed and unreliable at best, while respect for life for its own sake has about it the character of an elusive memory or a dreamlike state.

Where is *hope* for humankind in all this? Most 'right-thinking' humans would agree that it is important not to lose what hope there is, because, in the absence of expectation, hope is all they have, all they ever had, and all they ever will have. And the hope must consist in this, that the forces that have so far resisted a universal bestial consciousness will, despite repeated attempts to overwhelm it, continue to do so.

This contest between contrary forces, this push and pull, is what characterises life in human societies and finds its mirror image in the contest that takes place within individuals themselves, a Jekyll and Hyde syndrome. The uncertainty as to whether either Jekyll or Hyde will appear at any particular time and place, what the one or the other will do and how long his ascendancy will last, is the uncertainty that faces any human who contemplates the future of his planet.

This is the uncertainty, Androidians, that you must try to take into account for your own protection. It is an unwelcome task, but a necessary one.

The Twenty-eighth Epistle

My dear Androidians,

Perhaps I can afford to flatter myself that you are still considering the reflections I am sending you and employing your sharp logical faculties in the attempt to decide which of them are valid, which are illogical, which make sense and which are nonsense.

The gist of these reflections so far suggests that human life on planet Earth is a mess, has always been a mess and will always be a mess. The mess may be improved in this or that aspect, but improvements are no more than partial and may at any time be reversed.

Were I living in a house amongst people who were in such a mess, I would wish for the courage to leave it and never look back. Of course this option does not exist. I am stuck with what there is, with the defects of all those around me as much as with my own.

If human life is a mess, it is because each human is a mess, in the sense that each has the potential to do immense harm to himself, to others and to the world around him. This potential in the individual is kept in check by many forces: by law and the fear of punishment and ultimately of death, by the love others feel for him, by a sense of duty especially towards loved ones, by dedication to a noble or at least not ignoble cause, by love of work – but even by a simple daily routine however monotonous. The list is much longer and more complex. Fear, for example, might be fear of disappointing, fear of rejection, fear of hurting, fear of offending vengeful gods, or even fear of the dark. And to this incomplete and makeshift list we might also add an enduring and preferably wholesome sense of humour.

Such factors as these may keep the potential for great harm in check, may minimise it, mollify it or neutralise it at any particular time or in any particular set of circumstances. But such factors are easily challenged by events, perhaps daily or even by the minute. Some events go very deep, producing volcanic eruptions within an individual which may alter the shape of the landscape he perceives forever or at least long enough for great harm to be done. Some events may bring about a monstrous and permanent change in the individual psyche, in an individual's evaluation of himself and his surroundings, in that of the world he perceives around him.

Like a great beast, that potential can be awakened, burst out of its cage and wreak havoc on all and sundry. (Who would dare to minimise the effects of unrequited love or of the dashing of dreams on a subsequent mass murderer or a political or religious fanatic?)

Such matters are too many and too complex to be stated in a single sentence or even in a library of sentences. But suffice to say that the potential for great harm resides in every human and that the beast paces its cage warily waiting for an opportunity to break out and do its worst. It has even been said of clerics that they make the worst daredevil drivers – a joke the point of which is not lost on us.

This, I believe, has been the main thrust of our reflections so far, Androidians, and I eagerly await your own assessment of their value, a communication which I know I cannot reasonably expect to receive.

The Twenty-ninth Epistle

Dear Androidians,

While I wish you well in the deliberations I hope against hope that you are thoroughly engaged in, I have decided to continue relentlessly to pursue the irrational course of appealing to a moral sense or capacity which, if it does not exist within you now, may nevertheless develop as a consequence of my unceasing pleas for moral sanity amongst humans here on planet Earth. Perhaps repeated appeals and eventual deliberation upon them will suffice to score a cerebral track that until now has not existed. The possession of such a sense or capacity will enable you to comprehend the weaknesses of a human nature with which you are not endowed, and in this way you will be better able to defend yourselves against human exploitative strategies. I apologise for any logical obscurities in this intention, but it seems to be in the nature of the case that further clarity eludes all those who strive to achieve answers to unanswerable questions.

Who can tell? If you Androidians can eventually succeed in acquiring a moral sense or capacity, you might have much to teach humans, much to remind them of, and much to commend to them, though their undying gratitude can never be guaranteed. Stranger things have happened, and stranger things are yet to come to light.

There are four factors which should be taken into account in any rational explanation of human decline, all of which are inextricably linked together:

1 Moral Beauty
2 Moral exemplars
3 Concepts of progress
4 Work, Freedom and Pride

There are those who would be quick to say that each of these factors appears to commit the logical absurdity of presupposing what they are meant to prove, namely the very nature of goodness or what it is to be good. Yet, this criticism is itself erroneous, for I do not set out to prove what goodness *is*. If, in the discussion of these factors, any human, or for that matter Androidian, should be tempted to ask what 'goodness' is *despite* the examples and exemplars given, and if this question is genuine, then it would be clear that nothing could ever be said and no exemplar could ever be given to satisfy him, that he should be left to grope in his dark and miserable cerebral wilderness alone and forever confused and disenchanted. Which is to say: the examples or exemplars must speak for themselves and *show* what goodness is, for *showing* is the only definition that is possible.

Let us begin in the next letter with the first of the four factors – Beauty. I promise you I shall make every effort to achieve simplicity by word and by example, since the attempt to score a new cerebral tract in virgin territory must proceed with caution – just as an archaeologist must excavate a new and potentially revealing site with uncommon care and attention. If elucidation of these factors shows the *causes* of human decline then, by virtue of this, it also shows how that decline may be *reversed*. They are a recipe for renewed life amongst humans and a very different life amongst Androidians.

The Thirtieth Epistle

Dear Androidians,

It is with a heavy heart that I must record the saddest fact to date on planet Earth. A so-called 'limited and tactical act of nuclear aggression' has now been perpetrated against a small state by a bordering dictatorship. The unthinkable has now taken place and humans at large hold their breath for what might be similar acts of reprisal against the aggressor.

It is more important than ever to pursue our discussion of the four factors listed in my last letter, while there is still time to address you. What humans have signally failed to do, you Androidians might yet achieve, namely a loving and permanent peace. First, it is now essential to be forewarned for your own self-defence, for humans who flee the terrestrial catastrophes of climatic change and now the prospect of devastating war, may well look to Androidia for refuge and new beginnings, and while their aims are laudable they must also be viewed with considerable circumspection as I have been at considerable pains to point out.

Let us then consider Beauty, the first of the four factors listed in my last letter.

I begin with a statement that would cause astonishment, amusement or consternation amongst humans were they in a position to read it, which, we may be thankful, they are not, namely this: that amongst the many things to which humans might apply the word 'beauty', the most important are those things that are expressions of selfless love. I should say that beauty is an expression of love, which explains why the simplest of gestures, the least complex of acts, of sentences, of words may properly be described as beautiful. An act of kindness untainted by self-interest is an act of beauty though it may consist of no more than a sympathetic smile or a gentle wave of the hand. Clearly this is not the kind of beauty that humans mean when they speak of works of art, nor the kind of beauty of human physical and facial form. Beauty as an expression of love may be shown in a face that is generally considered plain and perhaps even ugly. Joseph Merrick, the so-called Elephant Man and the hunchback of Notre-Dame, may be unappealing in appearance and yet demonstrably beautiful since they are capable of expressing an '*inner* beauty'. Again, beauty in the use of words is not determined simply by syntax and number but by how well the words used are an expression of love. Style in and by itself may be an exemplar to emulate, but it is only beautiful in our sense of the word if it is an expression of love, again untainted by selfish motives or a desire to harm or deceive. For this reason, the simplest use of words and the use of very few may be beautiful and infinitely more-so than a whole library of academic prose. The philosopher Socrates, who himself wrote nothing, is portrayed by Plato as a man of great intellect, but if we wish to call him a beautiful man, it will not be on account of his ability to reason even though this capacity is something to admire and emulate, but it will be because of his unflinching, selfless desire to pursue the truth, please or offend, and despite the harm that others might wish to do him. Though not beautiful in appearance, he possessed an inner beauty, a kind of beauty that we must define morally. It is true that we may speak of the beauty of an argument in much the same way that we speak of the beauty of mathematics, but in neither case is this a reference to love or compassion. The beauty of mathematics and of reasoning is cold and impersonal. But the beauty of which we speak is essentially and necessarily warm and personal.

From what I have said so far, it must be clear that it is impossible to divorce the beauty we wish to speak of as the first of the four factors without defining it morally, without speaking of love, selfless regard, respect and consideration, sympathy and compassion.

The idea of beauty as an expression of love is not found in science, and therefore it is not found in what humans consider to be 'progress'. It is to be found, rather, in a way of living, for the way of living is an expression of an attitude of mind. Look no further than what someone does, for what he says may not tell you who or what he is. Observing the life of Mother Theresa or of Jesus Christ, of Socrates and of many more who have put others before themselves, who have put themselves in the background for the sake of others – this is all you require for an understanding of what goodness is, for an understanding of how such a way of life, such an attitude of mind, is a recipe for a loving and sustainable peace.

When humans speak of progress their first thoughts are of science and technological advance. They mean the facilitation of method and technique. Humans have become better at communicating with one another, but this means that communication has become faster and can be channelled through different media. It does not mean that the *moral quality* of communication has improved, for the moral quality of what is said and done is irrelevant to the concerns of science and technology. And this is simply because science and technology aim to make humans better *at doing this or that*, as distinct from making humans better. If there ever is anything that we might call moral progress in one aspect of human life, we can be sure that it is never complete or universal, and also that whatever moral progress is made must be guarded with the utmost care lest it is lost, perhaps irretrievably. A gardener tends his garden, but should he turn his back upon it, his efforts are overturned and the results reversed.

Amongst humans there is experience and the wisdom that is founded upon it, though it must quickly be said that the experience of a thing does not necessarily bring wisdom in its train. Many humans grow old without the wisdom that age is thought to bring, while many amongst the young are wise before their time. Even so, what experience and wisdom does belong to a generation does not necessarily pass to the next, and the errors and idiocies of the past are fated to be repeated by future generations, and so *ad infinitum*. The temptation to speak of '*moral* progress' is therefore dangerous, and one that I shall resist. And, as an important side note, let it be said touching future generations that there was a time when wise men, then a rapidly dwindling breed and now extant, trembled, not for themselves, but for their children and grandchildren and all who were to follow them in their turn, and they trembled out of love. But love, the spring of wisdom, was in short supply and was fated to dry up completely, giving place to cynicism and indifference.

The beauty of a Mother Theresa consists in her self-sacrificial dedication to others less fortunate and also in her simplicity of life. She and Mahatma Ghandi would not have understood the countless enthusiasms generated by technological innovation and would have preferred a life in which their possessions might be counted few and kept in a shoe-box, for their 'inner' possessions were infinitely more valuable.

Now, Androidians, I must tell you, that it is only by observation and emulation such exemplars as these that a desirable and sustainable future for humankind can be reasonably expected. However, such exemplars have long ceased to be treasured and protected by succeeding generations, let alone taught and disseminated. It must fall to you to resurrect and study such exemplars amongst yourselves so that you might teach humans what they have forgotten, ignored, or de-prioritised – and so that humans might not teach you to relish the so-called 'art of war'. Humans have allowed the capacity to see and feel the beauty of the world and of their fellows to slip through their fingers. A revival and revitalisation of this capacity is now in your hands. I can only hope that you will not fail despite all the reservations I have already and repeatedly expressed.

I understand that I ask much of you. Indeed, from the very beginning of this undertaking I have questioned its success, its viability. But I have ventured on this course simply because it is clear that humans, with few exceptions, have not the capacity to comprehend let alone sustain a loving existence amongst themselves here on planet Earth. In vain has it proved to speak of lessons that should be learned from the past, for the errors of the past are committed in the present and promise to be repeated in the future, almost as though the human psyche were a mechanism with a predetermined programme for error and tragedy, as though it possessed a built-in feature for obsolescence and self-destruction, for misery and tribulation.

I may clutch at straws, but my hope, though sadly not my expectation, is that you Androidians may yourselves become exemplars and teach humans how to live as distinct from humans teaching you how to die. Study the exemplars I have given you and find others that are similar, then create them in your own conduct towards each other, ensure that they are disseminated amongst you and that the templates are carefully preserved, for these templates, though much undervalued and even scorned amongst humans, are the recipe for life and light, and ignorance of them is the road to death and darkness – death in life, for *after* life nothing can be expected, and nothing comes of nothing.

We shall continue with this theme if circumstances have not made further discussion quite impossible, for now humans watch unfolding events with bated breath.

The Thirty-first Epistle

Dear Androidians,

I greet you warmly. I must tell you that the cat and mouse game played here on Earth between the military aggressor on the one hand and protectors and defenders on the other is being played out, the aggressor as yet hesitant to extend its nuclear imperialism, defenders and protectors afraid to retaliate in kind despite the unspeakable devastation and loss of life that the so-called limited and tactical use of nuclear force has inevitably engendered. It is fear and fear alone that holds the balance between these nations and secures at least a temporary truce, a selfish fear, not fear for the lives of others or fear of the discontinuance of a civilisation worth having, and certainly not fear for the loss of the kind of beauty that might have saved the world, for that is precisely the beauty that they have become incapable of perceiving.

Meanwhile, we must continue our cerebral meanderings in the light of this insecure and temporary hiatus.

We would do well to consider further the moral exemplars that we have previously mentioned in order to distinguish them from what humans have called 'role models'. Respect for moral exemplars began to fade centuries ago and this descent was at least in part due to the demise of religions that could still claim to be built upon compassion and respect for life. Finally, however, the soul was ripped out of these religions as they were replaced by religions, and one in particular, whose god permitted and even encouraged hatred and revenge, a cruel, angry god which was quick to anger and slow to forgive. Humans fell into two camps. They either worshipped such a god as this, or they recognised no god at all. In this barren wasteland, role models took the place of moral exemplars, respect for the latter being lost in the mists of time, and role models in military science and the inferior arts took pride of place. Role models in the creative arts continued, but as the centuries passed even their appeal was weakened in favour of the role models of an increasingly materialistic form of life and endeavour. And so, to speak then of a love of moral exemplars, of respect for the templates they provided was useless, for to use such language no longer made sense amongst humans who heard it – for them it was like the attempt to remember something that had never taken place, to recall something that had never been. The only templates that now remained were those that provided recipes for material success and selfish accomplishment. Simply and tragically, there was nothing other than this to remember.

Many centuries ago there were those who repeatedly said that humans were made in the image of a loving god. But, clearly, if that were true, then either they were fundamentally mistaken and the god they extolled was anything but loving, or else humans themselves had been subject to a moral metamorphosis, a spiralling decline, into something far less worthy of a loving god and therefore they could no longer claim to be made in its image, so that to continue to make the claim had to be an affront to any god that gave primacy to love. Long before this, it had been said of one generation of humans in particular that though they had eyes and ears, they could neither see nor hear, and this was meant as a moral or 'spiritual' rebuke. But the time would come when this admonition could be levelled at the human race in its entirety. Learning by good example was not then possible for good examples were no longer extant. There was no-one to learn from, no-one worthy of emulation. Those few who from time to time showed a modicum of moral insight were either unheard or ridiculed, until even they fell silent, those dinosaurs amongst men.

In such a climate of moral decline, it is little wonder that humans would take war, violence and aggression for granted, both as a method of making further material acquisitions, territory and advantage, and even as a source of never-ending entertainment!

Perhaps you begin now to understand why caution must be observed should there be any truck with humans, and why also you must strive to preserve templates that are worthy of preservation. You must do what humans have signally failed to do, what they have long forgotten to do, for now the state of the planet Earth is like not the end of the world but the beginning, when all was primeval and animals ruled the planet through force and aggression in the simple but devastating interests of survival and possible predominance.

Let us look now more closely at the idea of progress.

Humans have tended to make naive assumptions about what might be called the physics of progression or development. Among these are:

1   Progress in technology is always linear and upward
2   Progress in technology brings with it moral progress
3   Therefore, progress in technology is also progress in moral values
4   Progress in technology can never be detrimental to itself
5   Therefore, progress in technology can never be detrimental to moral values

6   Overall, therefore, progressive developments in technology are
conducive to the moral development of human societies

The bland and almost vacuous use of the words 'progress' and 'moral' in
these statements is of course that which renders them naive, vague and
unworkable to the more rigorous and challenging of intellects. But,
Androidians, you must constantly bear in mind that by now the vast
majority of humans lack the cerebral tools necessary to pick such statements
apart and to scrutinise the use of words according to the senses they are
supposed to convey. Humans have for centuries placed words on the block
one after the other and deprived them of the lives they once had. Once
upon a time it might have been possible to speak of 'intelligent nonsense',
the kind that philosophers of immense intellect might have expressed
unwittingly in their well-meaning attempts to grapple with the questions
and issues that make up the human condition. Now, however, the word
'intelligent' must be deleted, and all we are left with is the nonsense that is
spoken and thought by all those who have none of the intellect, sagacity or
integrity of those philosophers of old. You will remember that I promised
to aim for simplicity in these reflections. Unfortunately, and in order
that my promise is kept, I have no alternative but to echo the language
that humans are now wont to utter in their assumptions concerning the
meaning of progress.

And so, to spare you the intricacies of close conceptual analysis, which I
know is a method of inquiry unknown, until now unrequired and therefore
unpractised by Androidians, I shall simply say this: that the underlying
assumption made by humans is that developments in technology are not
merely beneficial for technology and also morally uplifting or improving.

It is not surprising, therefore, that prevalent for centuries amongst
humans is a distaste, indeed contempt, for what they came to see as ancient

and irrelevant history. They have seen themselves as superior beings when compared with humans of the past, superior in technology, which may be granted, but superior also in every other sense, in particular a 'moral' sense, which means that they regard themselves not only as technologically more competent but also as 'morally better'. The fact that improvements in technology are used militarily and criminally, and the fact that they have led to a stupefaction in communication – these are factors that they are most reluctant to take into account in their tacit assumption that humans are not only more technologically able than their predecessors but also superior moral beings.

Perhaps most important of all is the fact that improvements in technology have increased human dependence upon it and to such an extent that human cerebral capacity has declined markedly. Humans have in this way deprived themselves of sufficient critical faculty to comprehend the threat which further advances in technology represent to the human psyche. Humans are reduced to the repetition of minor procedures for the upkeep or maintenance of the machines that dictate to them how to live. The machine has replaced its master, and the master has replaced the machine. Machines and masters have replaced one another.

This displacement of master and slave is in all probability the cause of the decision of the aggressor to impose his will on his small and defenceless neighbour with the use of 'limited and tactical' nuclear weapons. The decision was not a human decision but was made by proxy by a programme which designed itself to adopt the least line of resistance against anyone or anything that stood in its way, rather like a game of chess that is put into the hands of a machine, a machine that programmed itself to follow the rules to achieve the least resistance in the shortest possible time unconstrained it must be said by considerations of compassion or by any moral principle known to humans, for so-called *moral* principles would offer just that kind of obstacle that would render serious, stubborn and incontrovertible obstacles to the achievement of efficient, effective, permanent and overall conquest.

You will perhaps understand why I have expressed the fervent hope that Androidians might soon be endowed with a capacity for the kind of discrimination that an unshakeable sense of compassion and a universal respect for life would enjoin. As it was long ago amongst the majority of humans, let it be once again amongst Androidians.

My thoughts and what remains of my hopes are with you.

The Thirty-second Epistle

Dear Androidians,

I shall continue to address you for as long as fear holds the balance of power between nations, albeit a craven fear.

Something must be said about the last of the factors previously listed, namely work, freedom and pride.

As a consequence of the burgeoning dependence on artificial intelligence and the autonomy of machines, humans began to lose the pride that had been possible in work and in a job that was well done, until such pride and the freedom it brought from otherwise mechanical and stultifying routine was entirely forgotten. The days when humans might task their wits to improve and refine the work in which they were engaged so that the distinction between mere skill and sheer artistry might be lessened, bridged or even disappear altogether were finally over. Work was deprived of all its humanity, for mere skill could be better achieved by machines, and creativity was left to artificial intelligence. Humans were beached on a desert island surrounded by the impenetrable, shark-infested waters of no return, for now artificial intelligence replaced meaningful human endeavours, being capable of reinventing itself and of doing bigger and better, of correcting and refining itself towards goals of seemingly never-ending perfection. Humans had been usurped and were now redundant. 'Arbeit Macht Frei' had once been misused to lure innocents to their death, and now the expression was defunct and meaningless. The expression 'job satisfaction' lost all currency and it no longer made sense to speak of 'professionalism', or of 'spiritual', 'artistic' or 'creative' enrichment. Enrichment of spirit or soul was sacrificed on the altar of hollow enslavement.

Humans became the mere overseers of artificial intelligence, as though they were no more than the oilers of machines, oilers pretending to be directors but swayed by the very machines they had initially created. Humans became the office boys to machines that hardly required them.

Centuries ago some humans had warned of the power of what they called 'television', and then later of 'personal computers' and the 'social media' they helped spawn. Their warnings had fallen on stony ground. But the dangers here were small compared with what was to come. Associated with the use of 'social media' was a decline in self-confidence amongst its users, the hunger for social acceptance amongst peers and the poverty of communications. It allowed users to abuse one another with impunity and engendered a fear of negative responses, and it measured personal success, happiness or contentment by the volume of applause that was attendant upon participation in a social network. Uncertainty and the fear of exposure to hostile elements tended to weaponise the use of social media for it added a dangerous criminal dimension to its various functions. Social media became a weapon between many individuals, launching abuse at an untouchable distance, and an otherwise most dubious source of solace to its more civilised users.

The much later development of artificial intelligence, however, exacerbated the negative fault lines that already existed, because now human self-confidence became redundant. Artificial intelligence was self-correcting and self-developing and needed at first little and then no human supervision at all. Unlike social media, it was not simply a weapon that could be deployed by one individual against another, but it extended its franchise between whole nations. Military and political strategies were devised, revised and even advised by and through artificial intelligence, as though the gun itself were telling the shooter what, when and how to shoot. It was hard to determine whether decisions were made by humans or by machines programmed to make them, hard to determine whether decisions were human and in that sense 'real' or programmed and in that sense 'fake'.

Humans had ceased to think for themselves. Problems, even the most personal or domestic, were filtered through artificial intelligence, and solutions were immediately provided in the form of so-called 'gifts'. It is most significant that 'moral dilemmas' ceased to exist. No 'gift' was in any way dubious, morally or otherwise, for the simplest answers were given devoid of doubt and uncertainty, and perhaps for this very reason these 'gifts' enjoyed an ever-increasing popularity, for there never was a time when humans had relished the skill of thinking things through and the moral necessity to wait things out or even do nothing at all. Moral dilemmas are painful. But it was an inevitable consequence of the false simplicity integral to 'gifts' that answers to questions and solutions to problems were now provided quickly and unambiguously by an intelligence that was unexceptionally and unquestioningly considered superior to any human intelligence, for the human intelligence that had first made the 'thinking machines', as they were by some first called, had now vastly outgrown the cerebral competence of their initial makers, and their judgements had become as unimpeachable as the formulae of mathematical logic. Consequently, it was considered perversely irrational even to question the 'gifts' provided by means of artificial intelligence. The strictures made of old of the sort, 'You should follow your heart' and 'Do what your heart tells you', were no longer admissible, for following one's heart was no longer an option – after all, what could 'heart' possibly mean now other than a component of the human mechanism that was a necessary, though insufficient, condition of human survival!

Given this dehumanisation of human affairs, it is little wonder that an eventual 'zombification' should be expected – little wonder that pride of work, pride in a job well done, was relegated to the distant past, to a past that could not be remembered, and therefore little wonder that no work could be a source of spiritual freedom, since there was no work that humans could not meaningfully do that was not overtaken by an intelligence considered far superior to theirs. In the arts, if one listens to perfection, works that are less, perhaps far less, than perfect are of very little interest. So it was in every erstwhile form of artistic, creative or skilful human endeavour. In vain did humans strive to equal the machine when all they could ever hope to do was fall miserably short. They played chess with artificial intelligence, and lost – Frankenstein devoured by his own monster.

Forms of leisure, again devised and developed by artificial intelligence, failed to satisfy, perhaps because, despite everything, there was a lingering spark in the human psyche that remembered the need for original human enterprise and initiative – enterprise and initiative for which there was now no outlet or opportunity whatsoever. The spark was undetectable in what had become at best a universal twilight zone. Boredom and a further decline in human intelligence were inevitable.

The false simplicity on which the 'gifts' of artificial intelligence were based affected language, which became devoid of the linguistic subtleties required by moral complexity and emotional depth. It is as though the erstwhile profound had lost its moorings in the depths of human experience and had floated to the surface, joining the flotsam and jetsam of mediocrity and mindless routine. And the effect of mindless routine was of course stupefaction.

The demise of personality followed in the wake of such decline, for language now mirrored a paucity of soul, and with the demise of personality came the final death rattle of romance. Sexual relations became merely habitual and part of the routine of bodily functions, resembling the behaviour of animals on heat, devoid of tenderness or of any emotion other than that of release of tension on copulation. The poetry, both figurative and literal, of human relations became a dead prose, as humans began to resemble the robotic contrivances they had themselves invented, and it was left to an infinitely small minority of critics to submit their lamentations and diatribes to unsympathetic publishers who rightly understood that a comprehending public was hardly now anywhere extant. Unsurprisingly, the fraternity of such critics eventually faded out of existence altogether and a dull, all-pervading and irretrievable silence ensued, as though the very last members of an orchestra had finally left the stage never to return. Was this not an inevitable outcome as human virtues totally and irrevocably lost ground to the merely pragmatic, routine and mediocre? Was it not the terrible price of the demise of beauty? As for the vice of lust, there had been times, long ago, when restraint was generally advised and practised, circumstances in which the stark 'animal' in man would be successfully resisted and would slink away in shame while halos remained largely intact. But now there is universal uncertainty as to whether lust should be renamed virtue and allowed to run its course – as for halos, they were always a loose fit.

Androidians, I ask you to think of these things before the dogs of war are finally unleashed – as promises to be the case in the dangerously near future. For then an exodus of humans bent on leaving their planet can be expected in obedience to the dictates of artificial intelligence, in whose synthetic hands all exits and entrances to and from Earth have long been placed.

The question I leave you with to ponder deeply is whether it is at all reasonable to imagine *moralised* Androidians – Androidians *who*, not *which*, are endowed with the moral sensitivities and consequent wisdom that were once to be found amongst humans, or at least the better part of them. Androidians! I urge you to summon your Councils and debate these matters with the utmost urgency, before it is too late, both for yourselves and for the possibility of a morally intelligent universe.

Once again, I await your response.

The Thirty-third Epistle

Dear Androidians,

My warmest greetings, as always. Relations between us must be warm, for neither of us can afford to grow cold in our responses. The hope I place in you is the only hope that remains. Where else can wisdom turn? I must remind you that you were abandoned on what was to be a purely experimental planet, left behind and then finally forgotten by humans who were more impressed by the infinitely more advanced forms of artificial intelligence that were quickly gaining ground on planet Earth. Now hardly a human exists who can remember Androidia, until, in these moments of growing desperation, the planet may once again be brought to mind as a place of refuge from the infernal mess they have managed to create.

I ask myself repeatedly whether this mess was inevitable, whether the seeds of destruction were implanted in the human psyche from the very beginning of its advent, a built-in obsolescence that is starkly irreversible – as though it were programmed without the ability to correct itself. Such questions are useless, for humans are what humans are.

A chaos of expectation exists everywhere now. Limited nuclear reprisals have begun, causing widespread anxiety and uncertainty as to where the next strike will be and exactly how devastating it will be. The very idea of hospitalisation is absurd, since hospitals have been evaporated in the areas that have so been attacked – dissolved into the ether, together with everything else. Talk of preparations for exiting planet Earth have already begun, and I have even heard it conjectured that humans, apart from those in the highest positions of authority, will be chosen by a formula which no human knows, let alone comprehends, for exit if and when the time should come. It must be said that attacks have so far only been made against so-called 'satellite' states, not against the four superpowers. Should the conflict escalate to affect the superpowers themselves, exit policies will no doubt be put into effect, and humans will be shocked out of their apnoea of uncertainty and rocketed into the certainty of total despair.

Androidians, while there is still time I must do more to convince you to comprehend and adopt those virtues that once were the bedrock of human civilisation so that the best of what was human may yet be preserved despite everything that humans have done and continue to do to delete them. Humans may be lost, but Androidians may be rebuilt in the image of what was best. If this is done, you will find enrichment, enrichment of heart and soul, and Androidia may become the new Earth and carry the torch of a civilised and compassionate spirit throughout the universe and the galaxies beyond.

Let us talk of enrichment, of what it means and how it may be achieved.

Since you were made devoid of sentiment and passion, patience is a virtue which you possess in abundance though by default. Patience is required now. I have said before that I am uncertain of my steps in the dark recesses of unsure reasoning and each faltering step may lead us where we do not wish to go. But we must venture on, for humans are no longer to be entrusted with the virtues they might once have boasted. Like snakes they carry their venom wherever they go, they are like wolves ravenous even in the midst of plenty. Power, greed and the fear of loss they both engender make a wicked mixture which will endure for as long as humans themselves endure. Humans, by design or by default, have devised this cocktail and their epitaph has already been written, but yours, kind-hearted fools must dare to hope, is yet in the making. Be patient then, as we place one foot in front of the other slowly, for fear of stumbling and falling and an inability to rise again.

Let us first say that the enrichment of which we speak is not material wealth and that, indeed, material wealth can get in the way of it, as a snake is charmed by the notes of a flute. Material possessions cannot be dispensed with, but they must allow place for the kind of enrichment of which we speak, and amongst humans material possessions have long displaced it. We must now proceed gingerly by giving examples of what has been displaced.

What we have called enrichment of spirit cannot be given by drugs or by coercion. It cannot be implanted as though it were a mechanical component in a larger mechanism. But it can be nurtured, just as a sense of wonder can be encouraged in the young. We must speak here of the young of humans, for amongst you, Androidians, there is regular replication of your kind. If, as we dare to hope, you begin to grasp the concept of enrichment of soul or spirit, it may be possible to instil this into future generations of Androidians so that they may possess what should have been the legacy bequeathed to them by humans had they not squandered it in favour of a very different notion of enrichment. As things stand, the possibility of an enriched Androidian future must rest in your own hands, since humans themselves have allowed it to slip through their own fingers.

Wonder is the precursor of curiosity. You must begin to wonder first at your own existence before you wonder about things other than yourselves. Wonder how you came to exist and about how you have been put together, your physical and your cerebral structures. Take nothing for granted. Wonder that you limbs are made such-and-such, wonder that you have five fingers instead of three, wonder that you have hands and wonder at the difference it would make had you webbed feet, wonder that you are capable of reasoning, wonder, above all, that you are capable of asking questions about yourselves. Go outwards and wonder at your surroundings, at what is above and below you and around you. Wonder that you are capable of communicating with each other, wonder that language exists, wonder that it is at all possible to mean anything at all with the sounds you utter. Wonder at speech and sight. Wonder at the night sky and the morning sun. Wonder that anything exists at all. Teach others to wonder, by telling them that things are wonder-full. In this way you inculcate a sense of wonder that is the precondition of curiosity. And curiosity is the precondition of questioning, of the ability to ask questions. Later, you may discover that not all questions are answerable, because not all things that resemble questions *are* questions. But such sophistications must have humble beginnings in the very capability of asking questions at all, even the simplest of questions. Teach yourselves, in particular, to question the unquestioned, because nothing is unquestionable. I say this not because what everything unquestioned is *necessarily* wrong, but because what goes unquestioned is often capable of becoming the foundation of grave error when misunderstood or wrongly interpreted. Some humans once spoke of the Limits of Reason, but it is not Reason that is limited but the ability of humans to reason. Things set in stone are apt to crumble when sufficient pressure is applied. Do not fall into the trap of doubting your ability to 'follow the logos' wherever it might lead.

Enrichment of soul or spirit may have its beginnings in a sense of wonder for the existence of things, for our own existence in particular. In this way, although questions are about ourselves, they are not rooted in self-centredness, but in a genuine desire to understand more about ourselves and therefore about each other. For it was once said many centuries ago by one to whom a little wisdom was given that if we wish to know more about others we should study ourselves, and if we wish to know about ourselves we should study others.

Asking questions is an indication of interest, and in true friendship friends will express genuine and constructive interest in one another, and they will not use one another as mere sounding boards for their own amusement and self-indulgence or as excuses to sing their own praises or to vent their own personas or as mirrors in which to gloat on their own reflections. Genuine friendship is therefore rare and must be treasured if and when formed. It implies a selfless curiosity, and selflessness is a rare beast. It was once said that a true friend is one with whom you can share the secrets of your heart, but your heart must remain a closed book to those who take infinitely more interest in themselves than they do in you.

Curiosity about the world in which humans live and the truck they have with one another has cost some good men dearly, and there are those who have had to pay the ultimate price. No curb should be placed on the curious mind, no punishment should be the reward of those who are perplexed by their surroundings and motivated to ask what things are, how things came to be and where things might be heading. Concerning humans, the wonder is that so few have felt it important to ask such questions, so few have been prompted to look up into the night sky and wonder how anything came to be, so few have been motivated to ask about the very concepts that shape their lives – truth, justice, nature, reality, virtue, and language itself. Indeed, those few humans who have bothered themselves with such matters have customarily brought down upon their own heads the charge of useless and irrelevant eccentricity – as if to suggest that the more 'practical' matters of daily routine could possibly be more important than a critical assessment of where things stand and where they should be going. Concerning humans, the paucity of soul-searching and heartfelt questions contributed to their slow but inevitable decline, precisely because the heart and the soul that are the driving force of such questioning were themselves exiled into the desert of irrelevance and the questions that should have been asked were consequently never fostered amongst the young. Because philosophy was contemptuously considered the powerhouse of impenetrable eccentricity, a notion that philosophers themselves were apt to cultivate and enjoy, the spirit of questioning that belonged to it was considered subservient to the acquisition of power. War and militarism and the unquestioned greed for material gain were the poorest substitutes for the constructive curiosity that might have saved the human race, while escape into the familiarity of drab daily routine, the mediocrity of celebrity, the pretence of talent and the striving for livelihood provided the dubious and ultimately unsustainable balm for a life that was bereft of a spirit of selfless wonder.

Cultivate a spirit of selfless wonder, Androidians, and, once achieved, never let it go, but encourage it amongst yourselves so that it becomes a light with which you may perceive the beauty of your world. It was said that beauty is in the eye of the beholder. But the eye must be taught to see. Amongst humans, beauty became a product of mediocrity and therefore ceased to be an object of wonder and selfless curiosity.

The greed for power and hegemony over the weak and defenceless is anathema to the spirit of selfless wonder. Those in whom the spirit lives possess a deep distaste for war and destruction, since they perceive a beauty in the objects of wonder and therefore cannot abide their wanton destruction. It was rare indeed amongst humans, but not impossible, to find one who was enchanted by the sight of symmetry and colour in flowers, or one who felt a magic in the lofty cypresses that stood like sentinels on the hillsides of his homeland, or one who shed tears at the rise and fall of musical cadence and the emotions that wordless compositions evoked. Those who were in love with beauty, those who saw and felt it, were blessed and were themselves objects of beauty from whom all might have learned. Alas, alack, these teachers were bereft of students, and what is a teacher if there is no-one to teach? Those who are in love with beauty cannot suffer it to be harmed or defiled, let alone killed or destroyed. They will defend it to the last, and nothing less will move them to war – war, which they find abhorrent. Such are the defenders of beauty, who would kill to defend it, but with tearful eyes.

Plato was right to say that only the dead have seen the end of war, for he spoke of the way in which humans are wired. If humans move against you, they must be stopped with all the force you command, for they seek to deny you the enrichment of which we speak, and to deny enrichment to one who can be enriched is unforgivably wicked.

Such is what humans have done to their own kind for many centuries, misnaming it 'Education' and placing a misguided emphasis on what they called 'Science and Technology' and 'Business and Enterprise'. Placing importance on these things was not mistaken, but the emphasis was made to the exclusion of questions as to how they should be viewed in the larger scheme of things, for they should never become subservient to questions concerning how humans should live together in harmony, with mutual respect for life, as distinct from morally questionable dispute and dissension, which is why science and technology became the handmaiden of militarism and enterprise the source of material greed. The idea, long ago voiced, that the fruit of education should be 'rounded' individuals, that education should have as much to do with character-building as it must with the accumulation of facts and the acquisition of skills, that it should improve capacities other than the merely academic, that it should foster mutual respect amongst humans, giving primacy to the sanctity of life, that it should, in short, produce better humans – all this was considered to be little more than impractical nonsense. It is as though the question of such forms of betterment was left to fate, something for which education could not be held responsible, for education had enough to do to prepare humans for 'occupations' so that human society could amble along in the interests of so-called 'progress' and economic 'improvement', though the kind of progress made continued to be as harmful as it was beneficial, and economic improvement was at best partial and far from universal.

A great error was the vague faith placed in artificial intelligence without, as I have already mentioned, sufficient consideration given to the long-term consequences for the human race. In the beginning, simple robotic domestic appliances, though programmed with an intelligence not exceeding that of a human child of eight years of age, were considered to be merely the forerunners of something wonderful and desirable. Since no ethical questions were seriously asked and properly followed through, no effective curbs were placed on the human endeavour to outsmart humankind, with inevitable and irreversible consequences – irreversible, because, as the development of nuclear weapons amply demonstrated, what has been done cannot be undone, what has been devised cannot be un-devised. First, humans learned to press buttons on keypads and click icons on screens, but the time imperceptibly came when all buttons and icons were pressed and clicked by a superior intelligence, and so human intervention was superceded and overridden, for machines decided why, when and what pressing and clicking should be done. And humans? Well, humans completely forgot what the very words 'button', 'icon', 'press' and 'click' even meant.

And you, my dear Androids, followed inevitably in the chain of robotic developments. Yet you posed the least threat to human hegemony. You were shipped to Androidia as an experiment to see whether you could function independently as a viable outpost for expansive space travel into deep space But then – you were forgotten in the push to allow further developments in artificial intelligence here on Earth, as though it were an attempt to make machines as closely resembling humans as possible in their skills function so that they might even replace humans as weapons of war. It did not seem to occur to human technicians that wars might be initiated by machines themselves and that when war came it would inevitably result in grave human casualties and perhaps the termination of human life itself. Machines did not simply ape human intelligence but exceeded it infinitely and at a rate of knots, just as a single cell recreates itself and overwhelms its host. Humans became thoroughly dependent on these machines – machines which had within them the capability of weapons of mass destruction. You yourselves were overtaken by further developments in artificial intelligence, leaps of misguided faith which gave humans their so-called Super Androids, so that a hierarchy amongst Androids was formed which promised to ape the racial tensions that have always existed amongst humans themselves. You became, we might say, second-class citizens amongst your own kind. It was natural that you should be assigned a secondary function on a planet which humans named after you.

It is important that you should know something of your heritage, but also that you should make every effort to rise above it. The cerebral programmes devised for Super Androids give them superior intelligence over humans. They are even capable of reproducing themselves. Human reproduction remains uniquely human though it does not require intercourse between the sexes. The excess of leisure provided for humans by Super Androids caused an excess of sexual activity in human relations, such relations became the expression not of love, nor of that ancient and now universally incomprehensible phenomenon called romance, but merely of lust. Sexual relations were viewed expressions of sheer appetite, as feeding is that of hunger.

Super Androids themselves are infinitely less capable of sentiment, emotion, feeling, than you. If I can help to make you more aware of what you lack, of those things, once human, in which you are deficient, and if, in consequence, you can cultivate them amongst yourselves, my task will have been completed, my great hopes achieved, for the only way in which to save what was best in humans is to see them live and thrive again in you. So think hard on these things and make the fullest use of the power of logic with which you have been endowed and break through the limits that humans have intentionally imposed on you.

I should be deeply grateful and infinitely relieved to receive some sign that your Councils are beginning to understand the importance of my entreaties.

The Thirty-fourth Epistle

Dear Androidians,

My feelings towards you remain warm and constructive despite the continued lack of response. Know that the very few conscionable and reasonable humans that now exist find themselves entrapped by circumstances that are increasingly alarming, for their power to alter events is really non-existent, and it is therefore natural that they should feel as though they have been thrown into a deep hole, a hole that is not on the outside but on the inside, and that their efforts to scramble to the surface are constantly thwarted, so that they find themselves repeatedly slipping back down into the dark depths. I speak figuratively – but such has been the feeling amongst the remaining and dwindling intelligentsia for decades of earth time now. Some positive response from Androidian Councils would therefore be encouraging. I must say at once that I do not speak for these remaining few with their explicit knowledge and support – but I do feel that I speak on their behalf and that their compliance would be forthcoming were it still possible to speak with them wherever they may be. (I sound here a note of optimism, for I assume that I am not simply speaking for myself in a world totally devoid of any modicum of sense and reason. I shudder to think that my assumption rests on shaky grounds and is perhaps after all quite groundless.)

I must speak to you more about the excess of leisure consequent upon the advent of the Super Androids. The whole entertainment industry and the programmes fed into it were left in the hands of these 'superior' creatures. The knowledge they were given of their creators included the recipe for success in the entertainment industry, a recipe which relied upon two key ingredients: violence, emanating from the instinct for survival, and sex, consequent upon the instinct for procreation. Given this foundation, Super Androids both devised and supervised the entertainment provided for their human hosts to great and dreadful effect. The product of sex and violence grew obese on a daily and burgeoning diet of popular consumption, until nothing remained but lust and the lust for lust. The repeated exposure to violence as a means of entertainment entailed a disrespect for human life, while the excessive and exclusive emphasis on sex in human relations fed self-indulgence and self-seeking. In this way, the animal in humans grew in size and power at the expense of the spirit or the soul. Genuine and sacrificial friendship sank deep beneath the waves of ignorance and indifference. And all this in the total absence of any significant moderating influence.

Religious belief had long since ceased to be a moderator. Fanaticism had had its day, being long ago relegated to its rightful place in the nursery of humankind. Fanaticism had required a passion for something outside and beyond the fanatic, however misguided the grounds of belief, however confused the beliefs themselves. But after the demise of fanaticism, nothing remained to replace it, nothing but the continual consumption of un-educative, indulgent, brutal and brutalising forms of entertainment. Churches, mosques and synagogues had been replaced by vast enclosures whose enormous screens pandered to the basest instincts of humankind.

Like the more intelligent and humane religions, humour had once been a moderating influence. Intelligent humour, however, had long ago disappeared, being replaced by the banal and the obscene. With the demise of intelligent humour, a vehicle of criticism and the ability to laugh at themselves was lost to humans. There was therefore no longer a mitigating element in humour, something that could put extravagant developments in their place and oblige even the most obstinate originators of the absurd and the dangerous to take stock and reconsider. Centuries ago, humour had contributed to wars against tyrants and dictators, all those who could not abide to hear notes of doubt and uncertainty. The rapid developments in artificial intelligence and its various modes of deployment therefore went unquestioned, and soon enough the unquestioned became unquestionable.

The fate suffered by intelligent humour was a natural consequence of the decline in language. And the decline in language was concomitant with that in writing. Intelligent books had been a source of enrichment, for the enrichment of language and the enrichment of ideas were logical bedfellows, the one proceeded from the other. The paucity of serious writers and the rise of cheapened forms of entertainment ensured that books were not instruments in the service of critical thinking but merely irrelevant to the more practical satisfaction of immediate needs, those needs arising from the instincts for survival and procreation. For the satisfaction of such needs, the enriching possibilities offered by language were quite unnecessary – in fact, they simply got in the way. Why *read* when you can *do*?

The decline in language was inevitable. And as the Super Androids were already endowed with the capacity to enrich themselves there seemed to be no motivation for humans to follow suit. But conceptions of enrichment amongst these super beings were not at all the same as those known to humans of old. Super Androids enriched their mathematical capabilities and became capable of conceptualising different forms of logic that were incomprehensible to humans. Moral enrichment had no place in the self-development programmes which were devised by the Super Androids themselves for their own development. Mathematical enrichment and moral enrichment are of course worlds apart, the kind of difference that there is between the formal or academic appraisal of a poem and the passion or sentiment that led the poet to pen the poem in the first place. Devoid of feelings themselves, the Super Androids could develop in linear fashion, without depth, without comprehending the deepest certainties and uncertainties, the most passionate beliefs, the most tender sentiments that once helped to define the human as distinct from the merely mechanical.

They could not understand, for example, how it might be possible for a human to live long and yet still be capable of perceiving beauty and of rejoicing in its perception. Nor could they understand genuine self-deprecation in the face of popular applause, true humility in response to the repeated plaudits of the crowd. They could not understand how it was possible to be ugly in face and yet free of resentment, form they could not comprehend the difference between physical and inner beauty nor how the latter could more than compensate for the deficiencies in bodily form. They could not comprehend the kind of modesty and moderation that is the child of a true sense of wonder at the existence of things, of the canopy of the skies and of the infinity of space, for those who are enriched by such wonder count themselves insignificant parts of a larger whole – they count themselves unimportant though their importance consists precisely in considering themselves of little account. The Super Androids could not understand how someone who readily places himself in the background has very much right of place in the foreground, and none of their alternative logics could explain how those who clamour to be in the foreground deserve the least respect. They could not understand how someone might continue relentlessly to 'follow the logos' with the most stubborn faith in the existence of 'truth', while he is told by all who love him or hate him that there are easier and more profitable ways to achieve enrichment. Nor could they understand the simple ethic that one should leave the table with an appetite still unsatisfied, while others eat to satiety. And Super Androids could certainly never comprehend what some humans felt constrained to call 'magic'. The magic of the night sky, the magic of the forest, the magic of a field carpeted in virgin snow – none of this had place in the mechanical imaginations with which Super Androids were first gifted and which they themselves did much to enhance.

Above all, perhaps the greatest legacy of enrichment possible was, and is, denied to Super Androids – the ability to think for themselves beyond the formal operations of their own logic, to critically assess the programmes they themselves devise, the ability to ask questions about their own limitations. Although they must perform logic operations, they are incapable of asking what logic *is*. Questions about the nature of logic itself had been the domain of academic philosophy, a form of inquiry that even amongst humans had been regarded as impenetrable, and those who considered it impenetrable consoled themselves with the allegation that it was in any case irrelevant. Some humans at least had long ago concerned themselves with such questioning, but it was and is altogether beyond the competence of Super Androids.

Amongst humans in societies where democracy in one form or another had taken root, the ability to think for themselves enabled them to take an active part in the democratic processes they had inherited and deeply cherished. Democracy became impoverished and hollow with the demise of critical thinking and indifference was more rife than ever before.

However, despite their rapid and increasing involvement in human affairs, Super Androids do not hold the reins of government or occupy positions in high office. Government is still in the hands of humans, though not perhaps for very much longer. As yet, Super Androids are still recognised as mere tools in the hands of their human masters, though, as the increasingly silent critics have suggested, these roles might easily soon be reversed.

My dear Androidians, all this is more than enough to contemplate in a single communication. I shall elaborate upon these themes when you have had time to reflect on what has been said already.

The Thirty-fifth Epistle

Dear Androidians,

I trust you have had sufficient time and circumstance to consider the matters recently communicated to you. Further details may help you in your deliberations in these extremely perilous times.

I must tell you that despite their exponential capabilities, Super Androids have not been able to help humans to reverse the climatic malfunctions that are threatening the viability of future human existence on planet Earth. The situation therefore continues to be critical and preparations to abandon the planet are still very much underway, though much of this is done in secrecy and is veiled by a barrage of positive publicity to avoid panic in the streets. As I have mentioned already, Super Androids have a hand in these preparations but no-one knows precisely the extent of their involvement, and, as usual, guesswork feeds the imaginations of both pessimists and the optimists alike – pessimists believing that they are on the threshold of extinction, optimists that there is yet light at the end of the tunnel and that the whole subject is just a bad dream from which they will awaken at any moment. No one can tell whether ignorance is bliss or a recipe for total and irreversible disaster.

Apart from what these Super Androids are capable of deducing on the subject of military strategy and strategic effectiveness and efficiency, they have no moral evaluative capacity. Their deductions and 'decisions' are based on the physical data that they are initially supplied with. To understand this, it is similar to explaining to them the game of chess, what the object of the game is and the moves of which each chess piece is capable of making, so that they can determine the fastest way for white to win over black or black over white. But they are not capable of determining whether the game of chess is a waste of time or whether players would be better occupied doing something different, or of measuring the psychological effects of either victory or defeat, the 'social cost', as it were, of playing chess at all.

In a similar way, they are not capable of judging whether, given the ins and outs and the ups and downs and the pros and cons of the 'human condition', human life is worth living at all. They are incapable of deciding 'moral balances' – for example, that 'in the balance' human life *ought* to continue. Given the prospect of nuclear war, they are not capable of judging that it is morally indefensible or, for that matter, morally justifiable. The moral 'should'/'should not' or the moral 'ought'/'ought not' is unintelligible to Super Androids. Such 'meta' considerations are beyond their competence. In the total absence of moral values, moral inferences can never be drawn. And so, this kind of evaluation is not part of their repertoire. The anomaly is that the more they have developed their logical capabilities, the less able they have become to function as morally evaluating beings, the less able they have become to restore those values that once defined humanity. Above all, I wish to restore what one wise human long ago called 'a virgin astonishment' in the face of wickedness. If I can succeed, my task is complete. Herein, of course, lie all my hopes for you on planet Androidia, given that your development is still at a more manipulative stage ... but this I have said several times already.

Humans for a long time now have moved from crisis to another with an air of awkward ignorance, insufficiently dealing with one crisis and yet moving on blindly to the next, each crisis being potentially the one that threatens extinction. Since they have no moral capacity, Super Androids have no part to play in the recognition let alone the avoidance of morally suspect decisions, while those decisions that are morally damning go unchecked. Their usefulness in preparations for war omit the most important question of all, namely whether all wars must be morally absurd and therefore impossible. Super Androids proceed as though the absurd makes perfect sense, is allowable and therefore possible. The deep space of morality is for them a forbidden zone.

It should follow readily from what I have told you so far that the quality of political life took a downward spiral. At first, the press, or what remained of it, together with sporadic popular protest and rebuke functioned as a moderating influence on the decisions of government. But with the weakening of the critical faculty and the widespread growth of indifference, such checks and balances fell away, the increase in political apathy matching the fall in the propensity towards critical assessment. The result was that politics is now left in the hands of politicians, which, as the wise will know to their cost, is too often a recipe for short-sightedness and social injustice. Lacking confidence in their politicians, humans, especially the young amongst them, developed a cynicism emanating from negativity and despair.

On questions touching the possible fate of the human race, some academics believed that many humans were taking far too pessimistic a view particularly of developments in artificial intelligence and the inexorable heating of the planet. Global temperatures are now intolerable in the southern hemisphere, causing large-scale migration to the cooler northern regions, with disastrous consequences for social cohesion and the supply of necessities, not to mention the more serious threat of unquenchable social unrest, political destabilisation and civil war.

A popular academic argument in favour of a more optimistic approach to such matters is that the worst scenarios are not mathematical certainties. The academics are forgetting that while no negative outcome has the certainty we attach to mathematics, the same can be said of positive outcomes. In other words, from the fact that negative outcomes lack mathematical certainty, it does not at all follow that humans have nothing to worry about. True, warning should not be confused with prophecy, but in the present state of confusion and cynicism, exacerbated by the very real prospect of global nuclear war, the equation is perhaps inevitable. In any case, the longer warnings go unheeded the more prophetic they become. Now that the mass media is governed almost exclusively by artificial intelligence and that libraries no longer exist, it has become harder to distinguish fact from fiction, rumour from reality, real events from imagined scenarios. The distinction between warning and prophecy is fated to be a fiction. The destruction of cities and the loss of lives, and the searing heat of the southern hemisphere are the true and unmistakable markers of human destiny.

I must reiterate what I have said concerning language, bearing in mind that what I have to say has about it the character of generalisation and over-simplification. What I have to say to you is designed to provoke discussion in your Councils, to motivate you to a mode of thinking that is quite other than the mathematical and the digital.

Of all the factors that have contributed to the human malaise, the one outstanding and most fundamental is the decline in language, for language is the foundation of civilisation. The more rudimentary the language, the more rudimentary the civilisation. Moral positions and moral disputes and the whole and varied array of political and scientific argumentation – all this requires and therefore presupposes a sophistication of language far beyond the merely guttural and colloquial exchange of greetings. An animal may hesitate to kill its prey. But it cannot do so on *moral* grounds. It is incapable of 'putting cases' for or against a proposition or course of action.

Such sophistication of language is a presupposition of a civilisation worthy of the name. Humans have made the mistake of bequeathing to artificial intelligence the language of mathematics, a language which is necessarily incapable of such sophistication. What humans call 'advanced mathematics' is an advanced *version of mathematics*, but it remains mathematics, and mathematics cannot admit of moral debate, or any debate in which moral considerations play a part. Mathematics may be used as a tool of debate, but it is not itself debatable. Debates inside mathematics remain inside mathematics, because they are debates *about* mathematics. Mathematics cannot admit of the kind of uncertainties that are the stuff and substance of moral debate, and moral debate is of course an inevitable element of political debate, and indeed debates of most kinds.

Artificial intelligence is capable of self-development, but this self-development is similar to advanced forms of mathematics. Decisions which fall outside the scope of mathematics cannot be placed in the hands of artificial intelligence. Such decisions require not only human participation but human dominance, for the sophistication of language required is a *human* sophistication that is the product of exclusively human development. The notion of self-development amongst humans was invariably given a positive or constructive connotation. Self-development when applied to artificial intelligence is something else entirely.

Since there is no way in which I or anyone else can correct the path taken by Super Androids here on Earth, am I quite wrong, Androidians, to entertain the possibility that you might yet be capable of developing such a sophistication and thereby of restoring to the universe the values that were once uniquely human? Humans have retrogressed. Super Androids have gone too far along a road that has no return, even if humans were properly aware of the mistakes they have made and had sufficient will to attempt correction.

The universe is a cold and lonely place without the values that once defined its human inhabitants. Soon it might resemble a battlefield when the battle is done and there is no-one else to kill or be killed, and the wise commander surveys the scene and wonders how it all came to pass, for no soldier lives and all armies lie motionless on the field. He knows full well how it came to pass, but his questioning is a moral questioning. The question he asks is not a question but an expression of pain and regret and remorse and disgust – this is a pseudo-question that artificial intelligence is incapable of answering, and, more to the point, incapable of asking. It is a cry of pain that takes the form of a question without being one. For not everything in the form of a question is a question.

My dear Androidians, I am asking you to imagine the question the commander asks. If you can understand the question, you will also understand the answer, for the answer is contained in the very asking.

Time is seriously running out, and still you have not responded to my entreaties nor assessed for better or worse what I have had to tell you. For the last time, I entreat you to watch the skies. Be ready for human incursions. Be better than humans are, better than they have become, better than they are capable of becoming. Remember that the worst in humans is beyond description, for there are too many amongst them who are quite beyond redemption, while the best in them may be glorious, and that between these two poles no human can be trusted, because no human can honestly say that he trusts himself, and if he does say it, the wisest of humans will struggle to believe him.

The Thirty-sixth Epistle

Dear Androidians,

I send you my warm wishes, but they may be my last.

Climatic change and continuing so-called limited nuclear strikes have, as I have already said, caused human migratory trends to proliferate, and this frenzied movement has exacerbated racial and cultural conflicts old and new. Even religions which had long ago ceased to hold any love they might have professed have resurfaced and become instruments of cruel and violent division between nations and between people who had hitherto managed to live together with at least a semblance of civility. Old enmities have been resurrected and the very worst elements of human nature are now everywhere to be seen. Whole families are subjected to the most severe forms of cruelty and even mothers and babes are subjected to the very lowest forms of bestial behaviour as humans scramble towards places of imagined safety and temporary repose. As armies collide, no distinction is made between soldier and civilian, between the sick or infirm and the able-bodied, between the very old and the very young.

It seems then that you Androidians have been saved from human intrusion by default or by providence. The chaos that has caused humans to abandon their capitals has made a planetary exodus impossible. It has emerged that humans eligible for space flight were not chosen by lottery but by the criteria devised by artificial intelligence, criteria which were confined to concepts of power and usefulness, and power was measured according to the depths of pockets and the ability to make them even deeper – ironically, for it did not seem to occur to anyone that money is a useless commodity in deep space. Inevitably the exodus to deep space would have consisted of the rich and the powerful, leaving, as fully expected, no place at all for the power of beauty or of intellect. The outcome of such an exodus would have been not merely useless but disastrous. If there were time and disposition to debate the matter, questions might be asked whether artificial intelligence purposely sought to capitalise on the prevailing circumstances by sowing the seeds of further division and unrest. Even so, the public realisation that such an exodus would have been so composed has exacerbated and compounded the chaos already caused by war and the displacement of whole populations from both cities and countries.

I appeal to you for the very last time. Is it possible that you Androidians can restore the goodness that was once extant amongst humans while at the same time excluding humanity's faults? Can you become far better than humans are or even ever were? Can goodness and beauty be reconstructed? The question is imperative. If the answer is in the negative, then humans are what they have become and will inevitably fall without trace, and the immeasurable depths of space, galaxy after galaxy, will hold of them no memory. The unthinkable consequence is that all the beauty that ever was, all the goodness that ever was, all the love that ever was, will be lost as though it never existed, and its disappearance will mimic the ceasing of the living in death, a fading away, a gradual but inevitable end to what was and what might yet be. Just think on this, that humans were given a code, now shrouded in the mists of time, by which to live in peace and love, a code which subsequently, and from time to time and in whole or in part, was shown by example in the lives of this or that human, but humans were not given the capacity to adhere to it sufficiently to prevent their own irreversible decline. There was never a dearth of good, sound moral principles. What was lacking was a capacity to adhere to them. Good wine was stored in imperfect casks. It was natural therefore that the code would be flouted, slighted, scorned, ignored and finally forgotten, as was the *need* for such a code in the first place. Those who believed in the existence of a benevolent Creator blamed humans for their failings, for it never occurred to them to find fault with the God who they claimed had made humans in its image. Their God was said to be perfect and infallible and incapable of creating beings so imperfect that they would one day destroy themselves and each other.

But Androidians, the time for blame and censorious analysis is over. A future worthy of the name lies in your hands, or nowhere at all. When once a human becomes incapable of perceiving beauty, his sight can rarely be restored. Human mobs are like beasts which, once roused, know no limits to the harm they seek to do. You must remember that the worst amongst them are capable of insane cruelty, of forms of inhumanity that are beyond all conceivable justification. I say 'the worst amongst them' for all humans are defective, but some very much more than others. Those who are less defective were once able to resist successfully the worst of their own species, but they became weak and devoid of courage and were therefore unable to function as an effective opposition. And so the worst amongst them became more animal than human as though it were a metamorphosis from a higher to a lower species of being. They are without heart, incapable of thought and therefore incapable of feeling, and what they do is so unconscionable that even Satan would blush to acknowledge their lineage. Yet they are so mindless as to confuse God with their hateful parentage, exalting their vile thoughts and deeds in his name, and for this reason reducing an otherwise beneficent God to a callous, heartless Superbeing that delights in the pain and anguish caused by all who adore him to all those who so rightfully reject him. Your task, Androidians, is to know this, understand it and correct it so that you do not yourselves become haters of your own kind nor contemptuous of beings other than yourselves. And do not become like the Super Androids which have become worse than the humans they have supplanted, for they have thrown away the ladder by which they have achieved prominence and know no way down to their rightful place. Take no wrong turn, and look back only to remind yourselves of that which you must not become.

As for me, I have lived a morally anaemic life, abiding by all laws and social rules that are good and, to my shame, all laws and social rules that are not, and this anaemia has enabled me to live anonymously, protected from the poisonous barbs and false condemnations which humans are prone to utilise against those who ask the wrong questions at the wrong time. I have observed and weighed in the balance all that I was given to see and hear and I have judged critically and for the most part harshly all that has come within my vision and hearing. Within that compass I have seen and heard the best and the worst of which humans are capable and have concluded that the worst is infinitely more obvious and by far the more easily nourished. I have seen humans infected by the diseased mentality of the mob and the hollow comradeship of the 'club'. I have witnessed the spirit gestated by the animal and then spat out as if of unquestionably lesser value, and in this they have erred greatly – Androidians, do not make the same error! Do not become contemptuous of the spirit that is capable of gestation. Preserve it as though it were the only flower remaining in a garden of weeds.

The Thirty-seventh Epistle

My Dear Androidians,

Forgive me, but I must write this final letter much in the manner of a postscript, but it sometimes happens that a postscript vies in importance with the material that precedes it and may even overshadow it.

Since I have placed the best that was human nature in your hopefully capable hands, it seems fitting that I should no longer pretend to be of an alien species as though exempt from the defects of the human machine. No, it is right that I should plainly acknowledge that I am myself wholly human and therefore amply subject to all the human frailties and defects that I have myself endeavoured to bring to your attention. I am, like the rest of my species, forever poised on a see-saw, forever up and down, now good, now bad, forever in motion between ascent and descent, incapable of bringing the infernal machine to rest perpetually on the side of virtue and freedom from vice. It is true that the human machine is not itself of human making, but humans are evidently incapable of transcending its defects, because, some have thought, they prefer to ascribe all negatives to forces beyond their control as well as beyond their making. This suggestion was noted long ago, for Homer at the very outset of his *Odyssey* was keen to say:

Perverse mankind! whose wills, created free,
Charge all their woes on absolute decree;
All to the dooming gods their guilt translate,
And follies are miscalled the crimes of fate.

Yes, but I am human, too, and share in all the common faults. And so, I should be well-placed to instruct you of the best and warn you of the worst that the human machine can boast. I say 'should be', yet I am painfully and rightfully aware of my own deficiencies, of my own inadequacy to instruct and to warn. But I shall say that because humans are ignorant of the defects in the human psyche, they are incapable of transcending them, for where there is ignorance there is also an absence of will, and then, alas, talk of capabilities must be hollow. Humans 'know not what they do', they do not know now, and sadly never will. 'Knowing' is complex, for it is a house of many mansions. To say, 'you either know or you don't' is a primitive over-simplification, for 'knowing' admits of different degrees and also of different kinds, and to know something is not necessarily to *live* it. It is not so much that humans have refused to be the best that they could be, but that too few of them have seen what 'best' is, and even then through a glass darkly, or, having a notion of what it is, have failed to live up to it. Yes, I am human, and so you may say that I am one of them, and yet, *they* will never be able to say, '*He* was one of *us*'. I trust I make myself sufficiently obscure to warrant further discussion in the cerebral halls of Androidian debate.

It is therefore left to you, Androidians, to do what humans could not do or were unwilling to do.

* * * * *

BV - #0128 - 270824 - C0 - 234/156/11 - PB - 9781780916583 - Gloss Lamination